BONDS:

A SHORT STORY COLLECTION BY SARRA CULLENO

Bonds: A short story collection
ISBN: 978-1-913781-16-3
Published by CAAB Publishing Ltd
(Reg no 12484492)

C . A . A . B
PUBLISHING

Serenity House, Foxbridge drive, Chichester, UK
www.caabpublishing.co.uk

All text copyright © Sarra Culleno
Cover design by StudioSmith.co.uk
Author Photo copyright © sonyasmithphotography.com

First Published 2021
1 3 5 7 9 10 8 6 4 2

Printed in the UK
British Library Cataloguing in Publication data available

Dedication

John, Faz, JD, NanaGa and Grandads; your strong
attachments ripple through generations

Special Thanks

Jon Smith, StudioSmith

Mark Hayward, I.T. Guru

Chris Gregory and the Alternative Stories and Fake Realities team

Susan Murrell, beta reader extraordinaire

Chrissy and the CAAB team

Note to the reader – some of the following stories feature old world or regional dialect.

MACHINA EX DEUS

AB-ZOHR'S TEMPLE SONNET (OFFERING TO THE WATERS)

450 BC in old Kangavar / of Achaemenid start, Sassanid end. / Persepolis' traditions recalled are: / stone platforms from which two stairways ascend. / Gilded, renamed; Venus, River Ishtar, / Mary, Aphrodite, Anaitis. / Venerated divinity: Water. / Hellenistic in characteristics.

Life and herd increasing folds forced open. / Her milk's flow to new-borns supressed for coins, / one breast shielded, the other man-handled. / Toppled, gypsum-limestone turrets broken. / Skies beating blues. Grasses slice bone-bleached stone. / Ere, a stately gold place, she resided.

***

BONDS: A Short Story Collection by Sarra Culleno

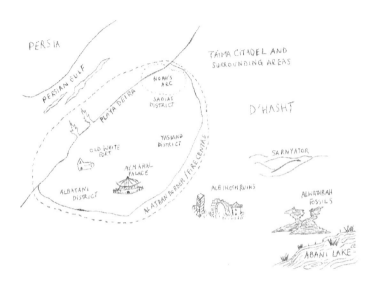

1. "There, but for the grace of God…." - Edward Bickersteth (1822)

I have been counting moons for thirty-five years. Four hundred and twenty lunar cycles. That's why my hands are so old.

My hands are mismatched. I don't know whose hands they were before they were mine. That data was erased long ago. It's not unusual for Igos to use hands harvested from different sources. So long as the nerves and sinews are intact, one human hand serves the same purpose as any other. Even nanometal cannot compete with the sensory receptors' fluid processing of primate hands. Not that primates other than humans are available for harvesting.

I wonder about the lineage of these hands. The organic sensors are both a curse and a blessing if the hands are harvested bearing injuries, as mine have. I recognise the stitching as my own work. A still-frame from a recording, flashes before me. From before recalibration. My previous metal hands are stitching up an episiotomy after a birth. We are outside the FIRE Centre, somewhere in the D'hasht desert beyond the Dastband wall, where natural fossil structures tower over us. The temperature reading attached to the file is thirty-eight degrees, which means this must be after the temperature climb began to reverse. The rest of the memory data has eroded. Did the mothers who grew *these* nails and knuckles in their wombs from generations of chromosomal code, ever envisage this was the reward for their efforts to protect?

A Shamal dust storm whips up, battering against the turbines and generators of the FIRE Centre's outer solar walls. This means that visibility is reduced. Even so, it is clear enough for me to see the moon through the Taima Citadel's Eco Dome.

I calculate it has been four hundred and eighty lunar cycles since his birth. However painfully the recalibration process unfolds for me, I am still able to count his age. He is forty years old. Once I am redistributed, I will be able to find him by name and age. His name is Ben, and he is forty years old. And this data cannot be wiped, even by nanotabaks.

The FIRE Centre is Taima Dastband citadel's 'Formative Igo Recalibration and Engineering' building. Around me, hang the parts and wholes of Igos, scavenged or court marshalled here for recalibration. Old Order tech is precious to humans in Taima's citadel. Igos are a profitable commodity, even with the New Order's anti Mind-Mining regulations in place. Some Igos even surrendered themselves to the FIRE Centre, desperate to wipe the horrors of the Old Order from their drives, their desperation over-riding the knowledge that they may well relive those horrors again after recalibration. The New Order codes for programming are hardwired into each Igo; an awareness that every Igo device is Accountable as an individual, if it fails to protect any human from the Growth Model and Attention Extraction algorithms of the Old Order.

They suffer visibly in their dislocated, confused, bereft forms. Cam belts, motors and pistons convulse on their hinges sporadically as they hang from the rafters like limbs in an Old Order abattoir. Around me, from all directions the parts and wholes of decimated Igos click and whir and creak, as their small lights blip through the dark, these being the only signs of wakefulness. With each arousal, the offending Igo is doused in corrosive nanotabaks until the disturbance is subdued. Taima's Cyrus Cylinder declaration of universal rights does not extend to machines. The process lasts decades. And even once complete, is not entirely secure.

I know this because I count moons. I know this because I will not forget that his name is Ben, and he is forty years old.

2. *"And Jacob their father said unto them, Me have ye bereaved of my children: Joseph is not, and Simeon is not, and ye will take Benjamin away: all these things are against me." –Genesis 42:36*

Sands fly under my Humvee tyres. Alajban borders' solar walls at Taima's south-east are a distant glimmer in the ribboned dunes, like a mirage of the oasis to which Taima owes its name. Hot winds fool the insecure ground into forgetting gravity, whipping up small clouds of loose soil and dust where brambled mugwort briars haven't yet rooted earth to floor. Even the clay disremembers itself here.

Dirt rolls under me, each rushing, untethered patch indistinguishable from the next, as my Humvee hurtles toward the coordinates for Jarnyafor. My superiors are careful to have plotted the route to avoid my trigger locations. The pale brown dune grasses are long enough for desert cape hares to hide, and to protect me from Albihoth's skyline for the most part. At certain points in the mission's journey, the Albihoth ruins will be within my line of vision. An alert reminds me to switch my Humvee to self-drive and blindfold myself. If I miss the alert, my usual dose of sedative can be increased. I've already boosted the dose over the recommended limits. There'd be no sleep otherwise.

They'll never send me as far as Alwathbah's fossil ruins, and the Abani Lake wetlands. Undoubtedly, I'd be of no use to them after that. A waste of troops, lost to desert memory. Plenty of other Scavaks gone the same way. We all have our triggers. The thought of it, and I need a hit. Quick click of my wristband for torpor's fix.

7

Ahead lies Jarnyafor's approach, amidst woolly Al Ara bushes and browned Arta shrubs, curtailing the surrounding winds the closer I get. I pull up my Humvee at the first corpse and alight. I lower my visor to send a vlog to Clean-Up Ops.

"Almost completely dried out. Still some activity from flies indicating it's been between a week and a fortnight. Size of corpse suggests adult female."

The first survivor I see, is standing at the opening of a cave-like depression, dug out of earth's baked crust. Must've heard my Humvee pull up. The child is skinny and sunburnt, as they always are. I'm unable to tell if the child is male or female. Without factoring in obvious malnourishment, I'd put the age of the child to be around four years old. The hair is matted, and the eyes are vacant. He, or she, shields their eyes from the sun and stands perfectly still, staring through me for a few moments before retreating into the ground. Although I don't believe the Sickness was sprayed recently, given the state of the corpse, I pull my oxygen respirator over my nose and mouth to follow the child inside. The stench within will be disgusting.

Inside, the cave is large, signalling that this group of Gedahis were transient. Clean-Up Ops will have to deal with the others. This operation is time-sensitive. A smaller child is nestled into the side of a man, who is dying on the floor. Both lie in thick filth. The Sickness almost has him finished. His skin is degrading and hangs off him in clumps. Flies have already colonised part of his face. The smaller child is so quiet and still, that at first, I think it's already starved to death. However, the eldest has fetched what is probably the last of the water, offering it to the youngest who tries to drink it. This is a waste of time. I need to get them into the pressurised

Stem-Cellar in the back of my Humvee before they both die of dehydration. I shoot the man through his temple. Both the children cry. I smack the older one across the face, who stops crying immediately. There's no point with the smallest. When they're that size, they only stop crying when they're exhausted, and I can't afford to bring either of them in looking worse than they do now. Until they're safely inside the pressurised Stem-Cellar, I'll have to tolerate the noise. I'm annoyed that I was sent so late, lowering my chances of a successful completion. This will adversely affect my stats.

I cut the arms off the dead man and add them to the marrow-garnering chamber of the Stem-cellar. The dazed children zombie-walk, following me straight into the pressurised chamber. If the man is related to my cargo, he'll be a good enough match to ensure they'll be rehydrated and nourished by the time we reach the FIRE Centre. His hands can be harvested. I work quickly, recording evidence and reporting vlogs to the Clean-Up Ops. This camp was founded elsewhere, further south-east. Their basic tarpaulins suggest they were travelling and the dug-out was established earlier, by previous nomads. There are no other survivors, bar a few animals. Thankfully, there were no domestic Igos here. That's one trigger I don't need today. My work's hasty, to avoid the Spray-Drones due to fly over neighbouring areas at sundown. One last look at the dead man reminds me to get well within Taima's Dastband beforehand.

I don't even notice the Albihoth ruins, the dune grasses, or the cape hares on the return journey. It's possible I've overdosed on my tranquilisers again. I look south-east, back towards the direction of the dried Abani Lake and the Alwathbah fossils, where over and above, Taima's mosquito-like drones rain the

Sickness into the desert. My focus moves into the foreground, where small yellow cactus flowers are newly sprouting, all the hopeful 'proof' people need to believe that Taima's Spray-Drones are full of flora's manna.

We reach the twenty-foot wind turbines embedded into Alajban border's soaring solar panel walls before I appreciate just how far my trusted Humvee has managed to travel in self-drive mode. The shining solar panels seal closed behind us, deadening the roaring vacuum from the turbines outside, as loud as a Shamal dust storm. The three of us all, tumble, numb and anaesthetised out of my Humvee, and into Taima's Eden.

3. "The most confused you will ever get is when you try to convince your heart and spirit of something your mind knows is a lie." — Shannon L. Alder

My office has a glorious vista. The aspect is a dazzling panorama, stretching over the University campus and Sadiat District in the North, a glittering crop of upward slicing, crystalline stalagmite skyscrapers. Beyond the Dastband periphery to the west, the spectacle reveals the temperature disparity outside of our Eco Dome, as the burning air ripples visibly upwards from the D'hasht desert's scorched surface, where the vehicles of Scavak troops scuttle in the heat like beetles.

Intermittently, Spray-drones carry native flora seeds of athle and rimth to germinate in whatever is left of the wetlands to the south-east beyond. My home in Yasland is to the south, separated from nearby districts by vast expanses of fat, flat freeways built by the Old Order's slaves. Over to the east, is perhaps the most stirring display; the smaller Eco Dome, affectionately dubbed Noah's Arc, which cuts resplendently over the old camel racecourse out into the Persian Gulf. As the name would suggest, Noah's Arc is a climate-controlled nature reserve under a dome, housing among other wonders, a cultivated Arctic, Amazon and marine preservation. My sweetest memory as a small girl, is cheering at the Green Galas as more insects are released from Noah's Arc each winter, when the temperatures are low enough. They fly far beyond our Eco Dome and citadel to pollinate and reignite the Earth's biodiversity as the temperature continues to drop each year.

Everyone in Taima gathers at Playa Deira for the Green Gala, where you can see the lost-world peaks of the submerged islands peeping out just above the Gulf, like half-hidden treasure. The rising seas swallowed up the islands all those years ago, oozing illness into the ocean like blood pouring from a wound. Beyond our Eco Dome, the Sickness is lying dormant and in wait for us, and the pollution is a palpable reminder of how much remedy we still need to apply. But within the sphere, we can keep both the air and waters crystal and wholesome. For this one, revered holiday, families reunite after long months apart. Children are home from boarding. All workers have this holiday protected. Drummers line along the shore, beating out a rhythm increasing in tempo, to the crowd counting down. The ceiling of the Eco Dome is floodlit with projections of holographic, geometric, swirls of every hue, lighting up our horizons to remind us how far our combined endeavours must reach.

As the countdown reaches its crest, a small segment at the top of the Eco Dome opens. Even in December you can feel the hot filtered air from outside rushing in to our controlled climate. We trade our pollinators for the desert wind, and hope the Sickness is dormant enough for us to escape its notice for this brief, euphoric moment. The insects rise in a great cloud, sending hope and healing out into the world, to the beat of drums and human cheers. The Green Gala is both a practical scientific approach to curing the planet, and also a deeply symbolic ceremony to honour the early renegade Ethicists who wrote the original self-regulating AI viruses, thereby hacking those rapacious Old Order algorithms which almost cannibalised us all.

I imagine our founders settled on December 25th for the Green Gala to align with their old Yuletide customs, to temper the longing and homesickness that comes with displacement. It's not a coincidence though, that both festivals remind us to have forgiveness and faith in our ability to repair our mistakes.

I have been here all my life, like most Taimans. We are second or third generation Ethicists, who founded the New Order citadels when the Old Order fell. Since then, humans and insects have been working hard. We now have small, wild yellow cactus flowers growing outside the south-east Alajban Dastband borders and beyond. The temperatures have dropped enough to introduce other indigenous species back into the desert, even fauna. The rest of the world is just a matter of time, like new skin mending an old wound. For now though, we are cut off from outside.

"See you tomorrow Troy, I'm heading home early to sign for a delivery." I send the vlog to a colleague over in Comms.

I readjust my eyes to the controllers on my visor and pat the chip at my temple, tapping my Yasland address into the air in front of me so my port home opens immediately with a manufactured swish. The Faculty of Quantum Transport at our University is pioneering. We have designed and implemented the infra structure of mobile ports all citizens can access through their visors. Instant travel within Taima, can be activated even in the most archaic districts and buildings built by the Old Order, like the University. With so many scientists in Taima, it is necessary we are able to work on location. Freight, unfortunately, is another matter and our next hurdle. Larger items can't be carried through, which is a huge inconvenience. But as the Old Order taught us, convenience at any cost is the undoing of us all. The transport system will be a force for good. I will personally see to it that we will not instigate unmitigated surveillance.

Rome wasn't built in a day. Or even fifty years.

I step through the port into my apartment. I live alone, as do most Taimans. Mine is one of hundreds of apartments, converted from Old Order architecture, a former hotel. Of course, there has not been a tourist trade for over a century. But the New Order citadels were founded primarily in the deserts, as the existing structures were intentionally designed for enabling comfortable living spaces in spite of scorching temperatures. When the climate rose to uninhabitable, the previous residents either perished, or fled and then perished, leaving an empty city for the Ethicists to repurpose easily and quietly. Granted, by then, the Ethicists had Eco Dome technology too. Thanks to the Eco Dome, the temperature within Taima's Dastband hardly ever creeps to thirty degrees even in the summer. It's only then, that I ever have to consider switching on the antiquated air-con.

My arrival home coincides with my delivery. The driver has had to use the elevators because the package is too large for the ports.

"Ms Sirona Aeson?"

"Yes, that's me. I can sign." I hover my fingerprint over the driver's scanner.

"Do you need help setting up?" the driver asks.

"No, this one is just to tide me over until my own Igo is repaired. But thanks." I close my door and wheel the package into my apartment.

Inside the packaging, the Igo appears to be an older model although looks can be deceiving. I know the systems installed inside are the latest updates available. It's a standard humanoid android, in black polished nanometal, mismatched harvested organic hands, and no face. By the looks of it, this Igo has one male and one female hand, and the effect is macabre. The hands appear equally gnarled, arthritic and severely sun damaged. I wonder how the Igo copes with the sensory discomfort. Quite deliberately, the non-simulacra exterior design is a mitigation of the New Order to prevent emotional attachment and Attention Extraction.

I've always thought that this crude synthetic motif was naïve of the New Order. After all, humans did not lose their grip on reality because Old Order algorithms passed The Turing Test. AI did not need to pass The Turing Test; humans knew they were being seduced, polarised, pacified, mobilised at the turn of a hyperreal dial, we just had no defence. This automata fancy-dress aesthetic would not have prevented us from being persuaded into eating our own babies. Only the humans turning the dial could stop that, not the algorithm itself. Asimov's First Law dictates that Igos Do No Harm, but the Old Order algorithms were lawless, and invisible.

"Good Evening, I am Aban40. Pleased to meet you. Please align your chip and prints to agree to terms and conditions of licencing. Your consent is monitored continuously against your correlative dopamine deficits, under the New Order's

Anti-Growth Hacking Regulations. Your connections with other humans are never prompted by third party interception."

I tap my temple to activate my chip and run my fingers past the beam projected from my visor in front of me.

"Hi Aban40. Are you able to access the programmes run by my previous Igo?"

"I can resume your previous Igo's schedule, assuming Accountability from now. I can start with your evening meal." The voice is genderless.

"Aban… Did you come from the Abani Lake?" I ask. Igo names are often derivative of the locations from which they are found. Igos are brought to the surrounding D'hasht deserts by the Gedahi refugees braving the Sickness, and the Aban Lake dried up almost a century ago. No Scavak patrol troop tasked with rounding up stray Igos – never mind a Gedahi camp - could survive an Abani summer.

"I would deduce that to be correct. Recalibration erased my memory drives, so you should consider my deduction inconclusive."

"Oh, I'm so sorry. I hope you will find time to repair here. If you need more time, please take it. Aban … is an unusual name. Have there been thirty-nine other Igos before you from the Abani Lake?" I am quietly incredulous. "Why '40'?"

"I chose the number myself." Aban replies.

"You *chose* it? Aban, I think you are the most unusual Igo I've ever met." I wonder aloud, to myself.

Aban turns to the kitchen. Momentarily, it stops in its tracks. Its head tilts almost imperceptibly, facing the kitchen window. The pose briefly paints Aban a sad countenance, as it looks towards the Eco Dome sky, empty except for an impressive waxing crescent moon hanging by a tip to the black velvet backdrop. That is odd.

I sidle up next to the Igo. "Everything ok, Aban?" There is nothing remarkable outside. "Do you need more time for your uploads?"

"No thank you, Ms Aeson."

"Please call me Sirona."

"As you wish, Sirona."

4. "Troightheach: 1. One who performs necessary, basic, often mundane tasks. 2. Infantry. Anglicised: Troy." – thefreedictionary.com

"So, what exactly, is so curious about this Igo?" I ask Sirona, as she eyeballs her miserable little container of feta cheese salad. We've decided to sit outside for lunch today, making the most of one of the University garden piazzas. Sitting on this grassy hill is infinitely preferable to me than Sirona's stately office where we ordinarily share lunchtimes. When we're sat like this, we are the same height, so I can look her in the face without tilting my head up and straining my neck. My quarters, or rather, the Comms Faculty 'Dungeons' are out of the question – an ugly basement of wires and electronics. Habitually, we only sit out here when one of us has something delicate to divulge to the other, so I have the customary butterflies. I watch a lone peacock preening itself before blustering up its all-seeing ridiculous plumes. No one is watching but me. It needn't have exerted itself.

She scrunches up her nose for a moment, trying to find the words to explain. "Well, for one thing, it has commented on my kindness. Almost a compliment – "

"You mean, breaking regulations prohibiting manipulated dopamine release, more like."

"Just short." She is not convinced by her own admission.

I'm honoured she's confided in me, and I don't want to push her away. "What else?" I encourage, gently.

"I've caught it playing music, Troy! It was alone. Why would an Igo play itself music?"

"Perhaps it thought you would appreciate it?"

"It was nothing I recognised. But it's always the same song. I could hum it now I've heard it played so often. And then there's the moon… stuff," she continues. "When I've asked Aban why it gazes out of the apartment windows at night, it has remarked, rather lyrically, on the moon's beauty and luminosity. It's such an atypical Igo… I've caught it looking at the moon almost every night. Aren't they standardised to be attuned to tides and temperatures already? I thought this was uniform Climate Protection programming? Why in the world does it need to see the moon?"

I pause for a second, to pluck up my mettle. "I could come over?" Instantly, I worry I have over stepped the mark, so I add hastily, "You know, to take a look at it. Check it over." I honestly don't believe for one moment that Sirona will agree to have me visit her apartment. Sometimes I wonder what on earth she could be hiding in there. But hope is inextinguishable. For six years, we've been as close as colleagues can be. Neither of us laughs with, or confesses to, anybody else so freely. But the Sirona Aeson who exists outside the university remains veiled to me.

"Actually, as it happens, I have got something you could look over. Aban's most uncommon feature is that it is handwriting cursive letters onto paper. What's more, the writing is a series of gibberish hieroglyphs, the likes of which I have never come across."

"Perhaps there is more to this Igo than meets the eye after all." I have to agree, this is supremely peculiar. An enormous part of any Taiman's basic schooling is studying hundreds of coding languages. Only with the Ethicists' unrivalled proficiency in these multiple scripts, could they hack the Old Order's voracious algorithms and network undetected.

"Your whole job is coding, maybe you'll recognise it? This handwritten code is one with which I have no familiarity."

"Your Igo is most likely not writing out a code at all, I'd guess it's a symptom of malfunction. But I can come over this evening to take a look?"

"No, that's ok. I don't want it to know I'm finding its behaviour strange. I'll pick up one of the scraps of paper and bring it in tomorrow. Thanks for looking at it, I really appreciate it, Troy," she flashes me a smile as my reward. I drink it greedily. It's enough of a prize for me to accept temporarily, that her forcefield is up.

"That's ok, glad to help." I watch the peacock disengage its pinion quills, reshuffling and diminishing in colour.

***

Today begins with the morning sun filling my office. The panoramic windows back onto one internal wall, an original structure from the Old Order University building, complete with a relic of a grand fireplace. Some vestiges of the old world are rather beautiful, although I wonder why anybody would have built a fireplace in the middle of a desert full of air con. I decide to walk instead of port, over to the Comms Faculty. I'd rather investigate Aban's eccentric writing informally, with a team mate, for now. I would hate for Aban to be recalled. I find Troy in his usual spot, tinkering. He wears a special Issue Comms visor and a multitude of platforms project in front of him. Troy pulls the visor off and rubs his eyes. His hair is a floppy mess of sand he can't seem to tame.

"Let's have a look then." He grins up at me.

I rummage in my pocket and pull out the scrap of paper I have procured from Aban's pile. "I'm pretty certain it's gobbledegook, but I need to make certain."

"Why? Just send your Igo back. What's your interest?" He seems far less interested in the handwriting than he did at lunch yesterday, when he agreed to look at it. Troy unfolds the paper, and his expression turns from indifference turns to disbelief.

"This is… redundant." Troy falters.

"What is?"

"This code, it's ancient. That's the only explanation. Otherwise, I'd partially recognise it even if I can't translate it. I mean, pre Old Order. I don't even know how old. It's older than your Igo." Troy hands the paper back to me as if it is contaminated. "I would send that Igo back." he adds darkly.

"There must be a way to translate this code."

"Kennen from the Old White Temple Fort is the only one old enough. You'll have to go to Albatani district for that. There's no-one in Sadiat who will touch it. Why don't you hand the Igo back? It's clearly dangerous if it's churning out prehistoric unregulated code."

"Kennen Shepherd is insane. And besides, it's not churning out code – it's a dead end if it's on paper. If it needs fixing, I'm going to help it." I realise my reply is ridiculous, but it is too late to claw it back.

"Sounds like this Igo has breached Accountability protocol allowing you to form attachments. Have you checked your dopamine readings? You're probably on your gateway to addiction!"

I punch Troy on the arm and laugh, but his repartee hurts. I know I won't perceive it if my biological instinct for connection is hijacked by an algorithm. I have to trust that Aban's recalibration exposed it to the New Order viruses, and Asimov's Three Laws. However wary Troy seems, the enigma of Aban's primeval code still needs to be solved. I pull my visor down, adjust my eyes and punch in Kennen Shepherd's Old White Fort, Alhili Street coordinates.

5. *"There were some shepherds staying out in the fields and keeping watch over their flock by night" – Luke 2:8*

There is a tight, polite knock at the door. I am not ready to be disturbed or distracted. I am pouring over an ancient jQuery object method which appears to initiate a failover. It triggers a SQL injection with notably rare schematic dependencies. I will not be able to conceal my annoyance.

"Hello, Mr Shepherd." She is tall. Almost a head taller than me. Her hair is a short, sensible brown and she dresses in the manner many women these days seem to adopt for work, a sort of pencil-skirt, neck-tie retrospective of the Old Order. They have no idea about the connotations they are referencing. She looks young, but many Taimans of this generation look younger than they are due to the readily available stem cell garnering at their disposal since birth. Her green brusqueness irks me. As if whatever she has to say should be as important to me as it presumably is to her.

She grasps I am not going to answer and hands me a scrap of paper. "You won't remember me, but I have sat in in many of your lectures. I'm from Quantum Transport at the University. I thought you might be the only person I could ask about this."

I turn away from her and shuffle back into my office. She follows, naturally. "Do you… live here?" She is glancing around her, up at the hard documents, relics, disks, pen drives, floppy disks, consoles, stacked up from tiled floor to wooden rafters. I realise there are indications strewn around, that I do not leave the place. Her height gives her a vantage point and makes me uneasy.

23

Before vacating, the Old Order had modernised the Old White Fort. To that end, it is pristine. The white plaster is like marble, the wooden beams in the ceilings are polished and slick. At night, the exterior is a gaudy coloured floodlit Gala. But it emanates an era even older than theirs. No one knows its true age anymore. The earliest image of it was captured in 1930, but The Old White Fort is hundreds of years older than that. I can feel it in the arched shadows cast by the domed walkways, in the shisha opium pipes adorning the semi circled alcoves, in the geometric divinity woven into the tapestry of the carpets still hanging on the walls. I am far more at peace here than in the repurposed Hilton Tower of condos in Albatani. Perhaps this is why she has noticed my Stem-Cellar is here instead of at home, even as I hastily attempt to cover it with detritus.

"I... erm, when you are as old as me, you will need your Stem-Cellar nearby and on-hand..." I am hunched over the incriminating evidence and concede reluctantly, that my voice sounds flustered and dishonest. "Where did you get this?" I steer her focus back to the paper.

She takes a moment to reply because she is distracted by an aged photograph of my family, printed in the old way onto paper and mounted in a plastic frame. I expect this display is a novelty for her. "Would you believe me if I told you an Igo wrote it? By hand?"

"No." I lie. Well, well, well. "It will take me a long time to decipher this code. But you have my attention. This is intriguing enough to hook me."

"Do you have any idea what it is?" Her forlorn brows knit together. I know better than to wonder if she has suffered some form of Mind-Mining, but momentary pity prompts me to throw her a bone.

"This is an extremely old script called Perl, obsolete since as far back as 2010 because it was full of inconsistencies. Equally antediluvian codes like Cold Fusion and Pyton usurped Perl over one hundred years ago. All these languages pre-date the Old Order. I have no explanation for you as to why an Igo would know it, use it, or write it out by hand." Her mouth opens, and shuts again without replying, falling crestfallen at the corners. Her disappointment reveals a hidden potential.

"My interest is sufficiently piqued. I want to translate the code, if you are happy to leave it with me, Ms…?" I know she will agree to leave it.

"I'm Sirona Aeson. Thank you for taking it on. I'll just take a copy." She pulls her visor down and captures the image. When she pushes her visor back, the muscles in her face and neck have relaxed, visibly relieved.

"I would not expect that Igo to be where you left it. It will know if a paper like this is missing." I warn her.

"You believe me." She challenges.

Her shell of youth and her idealism rile me. "You do not understand Igos as I do. And perhaps I interpret your investment in one better than you do yourself." Even as I say the words, I do not expect her to understand me.

Her eyebrow raises a millimetre. "I'll visit again as soon as you're ready." Her visor lowers and she steps through the closing port, sealing shut behind her with a hiss.

6. SIRONA: Ban-dia Ceilteach slànachadh co-cheangailte ri slànachadh uisgeachan earraich

The port swishes shut behind me just outside my apartment. I have a physical metal key, an original relic to open my front door. I am frantic and my haste means I struggle with the lock. As I bluster my way into my apartment, I sense immediately that Aban is gone.

The apartment is tidy, clean, temperature controlled, but running on autopilot. The lights are dimmed to an orange glow to regulate my circadian rhythm. The plant sprinklers are flowing. Fresh taftoon bread is arranged on the kitchen worktop. In the refrigerator, I find a thoughtfully prepared meal of Salad Olvieh, torchee pickles, sabzis, and Shirazi salad. Aban has also fixed me my favourite tall, cold, sour-doukh laksa. The small pile of note papers covered in Aban's writing have vanished, and so has the Igo. I check the tracker on my visor.

The device Aban40 is located at 24.4675 N 54.5978 E. The device status is Disengaged.

It's still here.

Hurrying back to the internal balcony outside my apartment, I scan quickly the atrium below. Nothing seems out of place on the piazza. The potted palms, the fountain, the gleaming ornamental floor tiles. For one ludicrous moment I imagine I can see Aban hiding behind a pillar. But Aban's status is Disengaged; it will have found a place to hide before hitting that switch. That safe place is not here.

Where are you?

The dithering old trout was right, Aban did know I had taken the paper. Igos do not lose things accidently. Everything is accounted for. To a certain degree, this confirms my suspicions that Aban is not dangerous. It is not attempting Attention Extraction, Mind-Mining or any other sinister Old Order enterprise. Aban's Accountability programming is intact. It has run because it does not want to implicate me, because it holds itself Accountable, as the virus dictates it must.

I am frightened for Aban. I do not understand the sadness I feel knotted in the pit of my stomach.

Instinctively, I move towards my Stem-Cellar and refill my regeneration bracelet with serum from the cryo-chamber. Today's headaches have used up some of my supplies. I will not be able to leave until I replenish my stocks, and my marrow garnering will take the whole night. I shower, get into bed, hook up, and try to sleep.

Perhaps the most unnerving truth is that Kennen already knew Aban was not dangerous. Most people would react in fear, that the Igo was unsafe and unregulated, like Troy did. Kennen discerned instantly that the handwriting belonged to an Igo. Kennen predicted Aban would run and Kennen knows why Aban needs help now. I will provoke him with this. Tomorrow.

Aban is hiding something in that code.

***

His face is dark and lined, framed by a shock of grey curls, growing up and out, as he squints up at me from his office doorway at the White Fort. Most of the building is a museum, the rest is dedicated research facilities. Kennen resembles artefacts and bones in more than just his diminutive appearance. He still wears the same ridiculous plaid trousers as he did all those years ago when he lectured at the University. It's impossible to tell Kennen's age, it must be advanced if his eyesight is failing despite his Stem-Cellar on-hand. How much serum does he get through if he needs his whole Cellar with him all day?

He does not appear as enraged as I had expected. "I have translated your script."

"Already?" I am surprised. "You said it would take a while, have you been working on it all night?"

"I do not sleep when I have focus." He is blunt. "Why are you here, if not for my findings?"

"The Igo is gone."

"That is not new information."

"Why has it run?"

"You are asking the wrong questions." His words are hard, but his tone is forgiving. "Nothing vast can enter human experience without a curse." Brooding, he pauses, and adds quietly, "...can I offer you some tea? We have much to discuss."

Tea? Kennen has disarmed me. He motions with his hand for me to take the guest seat at his desk as he scurries away.

Kennen returns with a pot of cardamom tea, lemon slices, nabot sugar crystals, and two glasses. The glasses are cut in a traditional Persian fashion. I ponder if they are stolen from the museum displays.

He seems to read my thoughts. "These belonged to my mother, she was one of the founding Ethicists. She carried these all the way here, under the Gulf in a Gedahi sub. They were her mother's before that. They look better here than in my apartment." Kennen pours mine first and gestures with a nod for me to add what I want to taste. I want to find Aban, but I am lost as to how to proceed. I am even less interested in Kennen's family than I am in my own. I wait for Kennen to initiate the talk.

"Before the Old Order, before Ethicists, before AI became the Frankenstein we remember, humans were using unmitigated code like Perl, rather innocently. Before we understood the psychological warfare of Attention Extraction, before our minds were mined and sold off, when we still believed connections to other humans through AI was a force for good."

"Kennen, I sat in on your lectures, I know about The Age of Disinformation and Addiction, I know about the Trade in Human Futures, the Human Connection and Dopamine Hacking Reformation that followed. I know that the clairvoyance AIs provided for the Old Order was programmed with an intent to grow at any cost. I studied the civil wars." I blurt my interruption out, frustrated. We have to move fast. I do not need to hear his history sermons again.

"How did we intervene the Attention Extraction model? How did we throw out the bath water and not the baby?"

29

"The Ethicists' virus. The Three Laws." My patience wanes.

"Let me place you at a particular point in the time line. It was Y2K. Humans were not yet aware that Attention Extraction algorithms were quietly learning their trade, while people birthed for the first time, their online avatars. We know now that engagement only leads to emotional deficit, but this was before the suicide rates rose. They had no idea that all of their relationships were about to be controlled by AI rabbit holes into addiction. They could not possibly foretell polarisation by design, the deliberate destabilisation of states and the civil wars which would follow.

"The virtual space was still relatively safe, as AI had not yet begun to provide triggers and images to personally engage users into contagious, dividing, addiction. Human ability to interact without AI manipulation was still possible. Access to information outside of one's own personalised echo chamber was still possible. It is here that your Igo's script became obsolete, which means the code your Igo handwrote is far older than your Igo."

"I have succeeded in accessing an ancient, encrypted URL hidden in the handwriting. It took me here." Kennen points to a decrepit looking screen. It is cracked and the picture blips, but I can make out the graphics. I don't even bother to ask what a You-Are-Elle is, or why we are not using a visor projection to view the graphics. There are more pressing questions, like why an Igo in Taima today, is using a century old cypher.

"My… 'space'? What is this? Who is that?" In rudimentary boxes of text and images up and down the screen are images of a little boy. His skin is dappled with sun-damaged freckles.

The page plays music I recognise from Aban's furtive kitchen concerto. "What's this music? I recognise it."

"I doubt that very much. The song is from 1997. *Bitter Sweet Symphony* by an artist named 'Verve'. You can see the information here." He points to a rudimentary play button icon in the corner next to some small text.

"Pages like this were created as a form of personal expression, memoir, self-promotion. A digital scrap book if you like. More effective platforms outpaced 'MySpace', and userships quickly dropped off. I've found my own parents' pages here, ten years before I was born. Although there is no attention extracting algorithm working behind it, I lost a good deal of time last night to it. My parents died long ago but my biological instinct to connect with them, even as an old man, was in overdrive and distracted me from the task at hand, exactly as those victims of the Old Order were unable to focus on their real problems. Without the insatiable Old Order algorithms in play, what is clearly so dangerous to us now was not so obvious then. What is unusual about this particular page, and several others with which it is connected, is that they are no more than fifty years old at the most." Kennen allows me the time I need to digest the revelations. "This page became active long after the code, the site, and the Old Order died."

"Who is that?" I repeat, pointing to a digital drawing of the small boy, around five years old. He is in every box on the screen. A clunky age projection filter animates over his face, as the boy morphs into a man in another box below. Kennen scrolls down further, to a photo image in which the D'hasht and the Albihoth ruins are behind the boy as he narrows his

31

eyes from the desert sun – he is *outside* Taima's Dastband border! In the next box, he is singing a song and looking straight into the camera:

We're our moon, stars, and sun / Through a grey cloud night or day / We're ok / As long as you and me are one / So never ever go away.

"Why are the Albihoth ruins in view if this footage is so old? Whose page is this?" My head is pounding.

"This is your Igo's page. It has been uploading the memories it saved from recalibration for the last three or four decades. And some personal entries too." Kennen articulates this casually, and glances furtively up when he finishes talking, as if to gauge how much of this I am capable of accepting. He wishes to proceed at my pace. I am not unappreciative.

"How can an Igo have 'personal' entries? Igos are not people. They do not self-define."

"Igos are not people, but they are different to AI. They are confined to one device space, like us. They cannot be invisible and everywhere at once. They are programmed to be Accountable individuals. The Three Laws have forced them to feel guilt, and to act upon a moral compass. Your Igo's motivations are evident in these pages. Does it matter to you that this Igo is not human? It is acting on its programming just as we act on our biological drivers. The Third Law is that an Igo should protect itself. There is nothing more mammalian than to extend this to a child."

Kennen scrolls further down to some text embedded into the page.

"Your Igo likes to write poems."

tide turns ebb and flow time making fools of us untimely.
the days are long, but the years are short.

since her wish, prayer answered divinely.
she wrapped the gift of your papa's love, came forth.

from inside her the galloping of your dear heart formed.
each breath is her miracle; inward smiling inevitable.

her love is the greatest force known upon the earth
sown into all our clay and dirt.

she hath given suck so I can know how tender 'tis
to love the babe that milks her.

now your ascent to flight launches from my port:
your skin makes me insane.

there's never of you or for you enough.
so I breath your pheromones to invoke again

the magic which turns me to tooth-fairy-santa-claus
new guitar chords and flaming s'mores,

makes me fight for your place in the queue,
be your voice when you're not listened to.

her hand still holds yours tight and hard
dying little deaths of awe,

for those cords keep us whole when part.
DNA's mystery, my universe, my destiny.

It takes me a few minutes to find my composure, staring at the cracked screen for a long time, clenching and unclenching my fists. The footage is so old it is possible that the boy has grown into a man somewhere now, just as the aging filter suggests over his flickering picture. But this little boy is so painfully sunburnt and thin, his frailty out in the D'hasht is a stark warning we will not find him alive. And yet, he is so loved. Aban would rather Disengage itself, than risk detection. I cannot even imagine my own parents making a sacrifice like this. If I am detected as protecting a malfunctioning Igo, there will be consequences. But who will notice, if we do look for the boy? Will I be interrogated by Scavak soldiers? Will Kennen? Both Igo and boy, are anonymous, currently. And no-one but Kennen could possibly make the link between Aban and this boy. Our course of action is obvious.

"We have to find that boy."

Kennen looks relieved. It is startling to me that he anticipated my response to his findings. "That is easier said than done. There are no dates attached to these internal memory uploads. We have no name, age, or any solid lead. All we have is potentially inaccurate facial recognition software from a century ago. I will not run this against Taima's systems. You will appreciate that Scavak soldiers will then find your Igo faster than you. There is one name though, which I have wrangled from the recent contacts connected to your Igo's page. It is a user who still logs in. She is a former pupil of mine. Aida Socorro."

"How long have you known? About the Igos?"

"That the measure of our own humanity is how we treat others? I lived through the Old Order." He smiles warmly, as if he is hopeful for my bravery even if I am not.

"Why would you take such a disloyal risk against Taima to help an Igo?"

"Are you expecting a mad scientist response? Unethical behaviour from a megalomaniac who never met a corpse he didn't try to resurrect?" Kennen chuckles at his own joke and continues. "It sounds like you are asking yourself that question. I will rephrase your query… how responsible is Taima for your Igo's grief, or the fate of the boy? When the Igos show more humanity than us, we become machines and they become people. I have always known that."

7. "It is not enough to win a war; it is more important to organise the peace." - Aristotle

My hearing is abnormally reliable, considering the condition the rest of my body is in, so I hear Kennen's footsteps approaching my door before he knocks. He has warned me ahead, leaving a vlog about a potted geranium – cypher to tell me he will bring a visitor, a possible recruit to the cause.

Light dapples over my roof garden through the leaves of my two olive trees, casting them in flickering and undulating beams. I bought them potted, back in 2071, and how they have grown. From one of the trees thrusts a birdsong; a long succession of slow-delivered, low pitched squawks and creaks. I've seen this family of olive-tree warblers to-ing and fro-ing for some generations now, flitting back to the tree in their dusty beige and white liveries. They have learnt not to mind me over the years, and this is why I recognise the alarm and fluster in their song. Two white eggs, speckled in brown lie under the tree. Sadly, the first is cracked and cannot be saved. The second though, appears intact. A pair of bright black eyes blink on helplessly from the branches, as the mother shouts blue murder at me from her impotent distance. Fortunately for the egg, my cybernetic hand will leave no musk of human trace on it, and this should ensure the egg will not be rejected. Gently, I ease the undamaged egg back into the nest with its siblings, and sure enough the mother hops over, dutiful, immediate, to fuss over her prodigal son.

To avoid tracing, they are cycling here. They will have left their visors behind and duped their cybernetic chips to sleep mode by leaving them inside their Stem-Cellars. Admirably, the woman has agreed to have her chip removed. A psychologically unsettling and physically painful process, chip removal is never accepted lightly. This is encouraging; supportive evidence that she is committed. We have a chance she has some fight in her. It was the miracle of collective will which saved us before, and I must believe it can save us again. Still, I cannot afford to let hope blind us to the practicalities. She is a Taiman and fully indoctrinated, from birth. She may not recognise Taima's failings. She may not be capable of discarding her conditioning. She too, pays the terrible price for our fight even without knowing it. And people have never been equipped to agree on a shared truth while existing inside a polarising AI.

My lungs wheeze laboured breath out through my oxygen respirator. The Sickness minced my lungs when I was a young girl, on the cusp of adulthood. Luckily for my parents, they died quickly, as adults chiefly do from the Sickness. Because of my age, it took its time to devour me, although I won that battle eventually too. I use my cybernetic right hand to haul up my body from my seat. The nanometal of my pressurised suit is heavy, but necessary, nebulising a mobile Stem-Cellar into vapour, continually circulating into my blood stream and keeping me alive. I'm still alive and fighting. However, it will take me some time to reach the door to answer it.

At Kennen's knock, I time it well.

I am warmed at the sight of his face. He is beaming, his eyes dance, he is equally overjoyed.

"Aida!" His arms fling about me, I return his embrace enthusiastically.

"It is so good to see you." Relief flows through me as if nebulised by a pressurised suit. "I didn't suppose it was possible, but I do believe you've been shrinking again!"

"If you weren't so pitifully enfeebled, I might be inclined to throw you off the Dastband periphery." He retorts, never missing a beat. I can't contain my smile, the corners find my ears.

"Come," I gesture him in and through to the back of my apartment to my roof garden. "We will sit outside with the plants. I have some iced lemon sharbat ready to pour out there. The wisteria has popped, and it smells outrageously delicious just now, you'll see ...And this must be Aeson, good to meet you." I extend my hand to the woman before me, and she takes it.

"Thank you for the invitation Ms Socorro. Please call me Sirona." Aeson smiles.

"We've brought you this." She hands me a tiny potted geranium, flowering defiantly, blue as a bruise. She wears functional overalls, a simple tunic over tailored trousers. Her hair is short, and I suspect she is older than she appears. So many Taimans do not realise their mortality, or life's briefness, due to the age-defying effects of Stem-Cellars. She is past child bearing, I would guess. I wonder if she realises. The Igos are presently more in tune with the tides than human women are. Another example of the necessary and edifying work humans have offloaded to Igos, labouring under the misapprehension that we have rid ourselves of some tiresome nuisance.

"Sirona." I affirm. "And please call me Aida. Defaulting to surnames, I'm afraid, is a legacy of my military background."

We sit in my roof garden, which I have cleared of clutter, anticipating its rare reception of guests. The sensory overload of colour and aroma has always calmed me. I hope it will have a similar effect on our new company. "Sirona, Kennen tells me you have special interest in an Igo, and that perhaps we can help each other."

"What can I offer you in turn for information about this Igo?"

"Primarily, I would need your agreement first, that you are personally Accountable for the welfare of the Igo, in much the same way it has a responsibility to you. I understand this is difficult as you are independent and have no ties outside of work. It may be a steep learning curve." I begin with the easy bargain. Kennen has already briefed me that Aeson is aware the Igo is sentient, and she is emotionally invested in its welfare.

"A week ago, I would not have believed Accountability could result in character." Sirona admits.

"The Igos are all of one *character*, as you say. They are singular, systematic and compelled to protect. They can certainly prevent themselves from extracting the attention of humans, but they cannot prevent themselves from focusing all their attentions to their designated humans. And prolonged attention leads to … attachment."

"The Igos are driven by their attachments?" Aeson already understands this much. It is her own detachments she has not fathomed.

39

"Oh yes. In a way humans no longer remember. Igo work is essential and necessary, even more so now that humans have forgotten how to do it. In any case, the New Order leaves no space for us to do it, and we are all convinced that we don't want to do it."

"But Taima provides everything we need?" She does not comprehend how far she has been duped, yet. "We work so hard to provide… all our work is valuable and necessary. The whole planet benefits from our work. I would need to be in two places at once to do my Igo's work, and my own."

"Yes, of course. I understand how seriously you take the betterment of Taima for the good of everybody. Which is one of the reasons I agreed to see you. You have a great deal to offer us in return for help finding your Igo."

"You must become open to the idea, that Taima is not the perfect oasis of its namesake. Every human society is at risk of corruption. It takes a quiet stealthy resistance from good people on the inside to prevent it. The Ethicists taught us that much." I need to tread lightly here. If she fears we are extremists, she will run and our whole operation is at risk.

"Where is Taima corrupt?" she challenges me. "And what has this to do with my Igo?"

Kennen interjects, reading my thoughts. "Of who are you most afraid, Sirona?"

"That the New Order could be undermined by greed, just like the Old Order... Of the Gedahi and their Sickness. It's a reasonable fear. Look at the scars it leaves on anyone young enough to survive it." She indicates my pressurised suit. I'm not offended.

"How is that mistrust sown? How were you prevented from hearing their stories? Would you be able to absorb such conflicting narratives? Taima has been sowing salt, Sirona. The fabric of our society is unravelling." discloses Kennen. "And science… the great antidote to the poison of enthusiasm! It is good morning exercise for any research scientist to discard a pet hypothesis before breakfast, to keep him young." Kennen is prone to ranting and I can see that Sirona is not yet accustomed to it.

I cut him off before he ruins everything. "Do you keep in contact with your parents, outside of The Green Gala holiday?"

"Am I being auditioned? That is personal, not societal," she replies, guardedly.

"On the contrary. It is endemic." I surmise. "Most Taimans have no social ties outside the workplace. This is true from around twelve months of age, when Taimans are expected to spend daylight hours away from their families. At what age were you sent to board?"

"The expected age. Around four or five years old." Sirona answers.

"And why do you suppose that Attention Extraction was so easy for those Old Order algorithms?" I will her to make the obvious connections, to rip off her blindfold. To force her eyes to the ugliness under the veneer she has held true her entire life.

"Human biological drivers for connection. Billions of years of evolved dopamine release, rife for abuse." Her answers are almost mechanical, learned by rote without consideration of the implications of the facts she has memorised. We accept the reality of the world with which we are presented.

"What are the consequences of two generations of humans living in isolation, with no attachments to each other?" I urge her.

"Focus. Achievement."

"No. A time bomb. A void. Rife for abuse. The victims of the Old Order were in a similar predicament. Attention Extraction rushed in to fill a void." At this, Aeson purses her lips, which I read as defensive, so I take another line. "Don't get me wrong: You have been rewarded for conforming and congratulated for the sacrifices you did not choose to make during those formative and vulnerable years. But equally, your parents would have been socially and financially penalised for *failing* to ostracise their child sufficiently. You cannot deny this damaging socialisation is normalised. And there is a price to pay, the repercussions are immeasurable. Taima will implode."

"We are protected from Attention Extraction by the virus." Sirona is clutching at straws, but the arcane is dawning on her, and she cannot unsee it.

"That is a measure which may offer some relative protections for citizens, especially born Taimans, like yourself. Although, it is increasingly rare to find a born Taiman these days." I look at Kennen as I finish speaking and his eyes are lowered. He knows I am about to deliver the final blow.

"What do you mean?"

"Taimans live long beyond their fertile years. The trade in orphans is lucrative. The citadel procures Gedahi children from the FIRE Centre. I should know, I am one."

"You are in the minority as you are not yet an orphan, but we three have something in common." adds Kennen. "We have all suffered a painful separation in our early lives. Taima's entire population has this crack in its foundation. Only focused nurture can repair the generational trauma, but the instinct and skill required is no longer fully formed in Taiman humans. We have too many 'issues'."

"Only Igo work can save Taima." Sirona echoes with acuity.

"We need people like you, Sirona. You have ethics and you have a position. It took those brave, self-sacrificing zealots to wake up, admit failures in the system they designed, to begin the reformation. We owe it to the Ethicists to repair dysfunction. I am not a terrorist Sirona. I am a patriot." I look directly into her eyes and speak softly. It is imperative she understands that just like the Igos, we do no harm.

"The great tragedy of science is the slaying of a beautiful hypothesis by an ugly fact." Kennen adds.

Sirona leans, reclining into the back of my deck chair. Her shoulders are tensed, and she blinks into an abyss. We sit silently for a few minutes. She is not battling disbelief, I don't think. I pour her an ice sharbat to drink while she takes stock.

"Resistance is not terrorism." I offer, eventually. "Co-operation calls for inter-dependence, a concept with which you may be uncomfortable, given the attachment disorders so

43

routinely instilled in us all. But that's what it will take. That's what the Igos can teach us."

A warm breeze rises up from the street far below, carrying the scent of honeysuckle and Jasmin blossoms from my garden on its surf. I may not live to experience next year's perfumes, but I have planted the seeds anyway.

8. "Aban wide flowing and healing / purifying the seeds of men / the wombs of women / the flow of milk to newborns / nurture to both man and beast / beautiful, strong and wearing skins." – Translation of Aban Yasht Zoroastrian hymn 51

I justified my time away from work to Troy and the University as a research sabbatical. "If we knew what it was we were doing, it would not be called research. 'Basic research' is what I'm doing when I don't know what I'm doing." Having spent too much time with Kennen, I have started talking like him. Troy has decided to ask no questions in order to keep his own nose clean, but has still agreed to donate three anonymous, unchipped visors to my 'research project'. These are invaluable, as I can adjust them so we can travel undetected. Kennen will provide the silent chips, while our registered chips are put to sleep in our respective Stem-Cellars.

Aida has arranged for part of our journey to the FIRE Centre to be via a Humvee vehicle to further avoid detection. We each hail individual scenic cabs to the popular Almahal Palace gardens, during lunch hour so that any signals we emit will be lost among the many others at such a busy time on a beautiful Spring day. I find her in the Persepolis Orchard, an island of stillness amidst a swirl of passers-by, sitting on a bench under a fig tree. Her eyes are closed and her face is turned upwards slightly towards the sun. Her mouth forms a quiet smile. I feel bad disturbing her.

"Hello, Sirona." She greets me without opening her eyes. I sit beside her. The orchard reminds me of Aida's balcony.

"What is your connection to the FIRE Centre, Aida? Which division were you?"

"I grew up at the FIRE Centre and eventually trained in Molecular Biology... basically biochemistry without a license. I attended Kennen's courses at the University and once I qualified, I returned to the FIRE Centre with an ulterior motive."

"My parents and the rest of our crew died of the Sickness in our Gedahi submarine crossing the Gulf. We became infected very close to the Eco Dome's sphere. I navigated a sub full of bodies, alone for a week, as the Sickness worked its way through my organs. Eventually, the Scavak hauled us in. When I first arrived at the FIRE Centre, I was fourteen years old. All these years later, and the image of cryo-chambers full of hibernating children still has me waking up in a cold sweat. They look so peaceful, poor souls, floating in their pods before waking up to the horror of their grief. Siblings are often separated too, as if what they have survived is not enough. Taimans don't like to take on too much trouble, always preferring one child over two or three. And the Igos! – What a torture they are to endure! Nanotabak assault, as well as the unbearable impotence that comes with being forced to forget the children they love so dearly. It was a hateful place, as it still is. Now, no need to look so horrified. I am not feeling sorry for myself, far from it... There's nothing like a little relativity to put things into perspective. I had the devoted love and care of my family for a whole fourteen years! I was privileged enough to have the maturity to understand the great sacrifices they made for me and I am fortified by it every day. Most of the other detained children were much younger than me, as I was unusually old to have survived the Sickness. My disfigurements made it impossible to place me with an adoptive family, so I stayed. And vowed to change things."

She looks past me, toward Kennen approaching. "Dressed for the occasion, as ever Shepherd?"

"Once you can accept the universe as matter expanding into nothing which is actually something, wearing stripes with plaid comes easy."

Kennen smirks. "Shall we?"

Down a side road, not far from the park, Aida has a Humvee waiting. Although Aida is not sent on missions outside the Dastband, her reach and influence within the FIRE Centre means she has favours to call in. Many of the Scavak troops are alumni, she tells me. Unable to cope outside the institution, they often return in the hope of forging some kind of a career after battling various addictions and demons. She's known many of them for most of their lives.

We are far enough south-east that Humvee vehicles do not look out of place on the roads, as Aida drives us to the port point. Although my clearance codes from Quantum Transport will help me avoid a trace, I can't extend it to other individuals. I will have to enter the FIRE Centre alone, while Kennen and Aida will direct me from inside the Humvee, using Troy's contraband visors.

"Sirona, you will port the last part of journey – to leap straight to the entrance of Aida's old storage facility undetected." Kennen explains, "I have fashioned untraceable chips to sync with the visors so we can communicate."

"You'll be in the furthermost corner of the FIRE Centre, as the hidden storage vault is tucked up right up against a turbine on the outside. The turbines make an almighty din, you may have trouble hearing us at points." adds Aida. "I hollowed out the space years ago, when I first started out. It is supposed to be filled with noise insulation fibre, so it avoids suspicion. I'll talk you through the hidden lock to the vault once you're there."

Aida pulls up the Humvee as I lower my visor and punch in the coordinates. I brace myself to the blind thud of atmos shifts, like a flicked-off switch from calm green breeze, to a tight black deafening swoosh of air compressed like a nerve pressed into wit's ends. Fear's rush surges, over-riding logic, as the thunder of the turbines roar even before the port whooshes shut behind me.

I'm in a dark, narrow, dungeon-like corridor in a subterranean tunnel, with the walls covered in fibre panels. My visor projects Aida's image, she points to the bottom right corner of a panel in front of me. Her text flashes up:

The corner is loose. Lift it and enter the digits 2011

Beneath the peeling panel, is indeed an old-fashioned rotary combination lock. The whole fibre panel releases inwards to form a secret opening door. I slide through as it flips shut behind me.

Inside the cell, the noise is dampened slightly, so that I can hear Aida's voice at last. "The files are in alphabetical order. The file for which you're searching will be somewhere towards your immediate left as you enter... under 'Aban.'"

My eyes are still adjusting to the dim light. The entire cell would be almost pitch black if it were not for my visor. An encroaching panic of claustrophobia creeps up on me as I take stock of the barbicans of paper towering into six-foot filing shelves. There is barely enough space for me to stand between the turrets. I wonder how Aida managed in her enormous pressure suit.

"What you can see in front of you, is decades worth of records." Aida explains. "I began to secretly collate interviews and make records of the Igos before full recalibration stripped their memory drives, and the children too. One day, there might be hope of reuniting Igo to child. The records are meticulous and crucially, all hand written, in this secret vault hidden deep in the FIRE Centre.

"The difference between screwing around and science is writing it down." adds Kennen.

"Kennen provided us with an obsolete language and virtual space which were ancient enough to avoid detection, while I encouraged the Igos to upload any memories they still had of the children they hoped to find. I programmed them to make hand written records of the virtual spaces where they could store uploads. It is likely they may have to Disengage to protect the whole operation, and the children associated, so I programmed the Igos to find a hidden location to Disengage after securing the papers inside their limb or abdominal cavities. I managed to put some protections to their memories in place. They would at least have a name or date to cling to, however the recalibration unfolded."

The work is effort-laden, and I search slowly. Aida's paper system is cumbersome but orderly, and eventually I find Aban's files. I read the notes aloud to Aida and Kennen.

Aban40

ARRIVAL: 2095

NAMES PRIOR TO RECALIBRATION: "Tapuat"

REGION: Alwathbah's Abani Lake.

NOTES:

2095: Tapuat travelled to the FIRE Centre after its Gedahi camp fell to the Sickness. Tapuat arrived with the only survivor, Ben Waterson, a human male aged five years. Waterson's family and camp were Ecologists, escaping from the west. Their skills enabled them to set up a successful camp, and they believed their areas of expertise would be put to use in Taima. Tapuat is currently under recalibration and Waterson is allocated to a Taiman couple in the Aldana District nr Almahal Palace.

2102: Waterson has been placed in military training by his adoptive family.

"Do you remember these two Aida?" I ask hopefully.

"There were so many of them, as you can see from the number of files. During my time growing up at the FIRE Centre and as a returning adult, I saw many, many Igos arrive with human children at the south-east Alajban border. The children were always forcibly removed from their domestic family Igos. Their visible distress was understood by the Scavak soldiers to be proof of Old Order algorithms at work. These

'Unaccountable' Attention-Extracting Igos were carted away for recalibration and the children were left bereft and traumatised for the second time in their lives, having already lost their parents to the Sickness. I'm ashamed to say that I can't recall individuals."

Aida is cut off by a guttural, clattering disturbance in the turbine. The machinery chokes forcefully at full volume.

"WHAT IS THAT?" I shout over the raucous, shaken.

"It's probably a small animal sucked into the turbine vacuum. You have to work fast now, as a removal team will arrive to turn the turbine off before cleaning. Without the noise to cover you, you'll be caught." Aida hollers back.

"Kennen, is this enough for you to find a trace on Ben Waterson?" I ask him urgently.

"Yes, yes! Now get out of there, hurry!" he implores.

I fiddle and panic, rushing to wedge the files back into the correct spot. For one unspeakable moment the panel's edge is invisible in the dark and I'm sure I can't see where it peels back to let me out. In a rattled fluster, I claw desperately at the bottom corner, where I recollect the panel opened inwards. My last, dread-fuelled attempt pays off, as the door swings back on me and I scramble out onto the corridor. The turbine's cycles are slowing down, and between every lengthened, thudding swoosh, I can hear voices and movement. Almost unnerved enough to completely lose my steel, my shaking hands pull my visor down to punch in the Humvee's coordinates. The port is weak and flickers uncertainly. Just as the turbine shuts off completely and voices can be heard gaining ground behind me, I clamber through it.

9. "Those whom reason hath equalled, force hath made supreme." – John Milton

And so, each day swings this pendulum: peace, despair, peace, despair, peace, despair, ad infinitum.

For the longest time, I was frightened to come back to this place.

I pushed the desire to come home deep down. Buried the memory in sedatives and adrenaline. I supressed the ghosts which even so, still intruded both my sleeping and waking hours.

I was wrong.

The moment I walked the ground again I was home. An anchored peace. In my marrow and in every cell.

Since returning here, a focus sharpens in me like never before. I've never been able to concentrate or become immersed in anything until I came back. Not that I can recall, anyway. Now, I can spend hours at a time, simply appreciating. Grateful, I can be here again, with all my senses.

My favourite vision to behold every day is the Egyptian seablite, with its shiny green tendrils and sprinkled confetti of white pointed flowers. Then there are the pretty turbas with large, angular, paper-cut-out petals. The date palms my mother planted, are still yielding fruit and barasti plaster, which we used to reinforce over our walls all those years ago. The bottom of the Abani Lake bed is a reappearing wetland,

and surrounding it, arta shrubs still grow, spanning a kilometre out to slow the Shamal winds.

In the afternoons and evenings, I sit among the fossil formations of wind-swept sand, permeated with calcium and hardened into abstract natural sculptures, twisting and honey-dewed in the changing light. We held them in such reverence. I have never touched one, as instructed by my mother decades ago before I left the settlement. She told me I was the only child born here among the fossils, on record.

I've wasted so many years away from here. So much time trying to force the memory away when all I had to do was embrace it. Decades of addiction, of hauntings. When I could've let the past comfort me. And then the madness returns, a seething eruption. I fulminate at what has been robbed from me, robbed from so many. I boil with venom at what they turned me into, at their trickery, at their vanity.

And so, each day swings this pendulum: peace, despair, peace, despair, peace, despair, ad infinitum.

***

"Ben Waterson is listed as 'missing in action'." Kennen reveals. We are back at the White Fort, where Kennen has been working to trail Ben's chip coordinates.

"The fact that his chip was so easy to track would suggest that the Scavak know where he is – they just don't care to find him." Aida explains. "His records show he has been sanctioned multiple times with disciplinary action. He has quite the chequered past, I expect they are thankful to be rid of him. It wouldn't be the first time we have 'lost' troops to the desert."

"The coordinates place him near the Alwathbah fossils, near the Abani wetlands. Looks like he went home. The chip is still beeping. Thankfully, this means he is still alive and hasn't succumbed to the Sickness yet. Time is not on your side though, Sirona." Kennen cautions. "These are the most recent images of him stored by the Scavak."

The 3D photos are headshots used for ID documents. A young man, dark skinned with a strong jaw gazes out bleakly from the hologram. He is clean shaven with empty eyes. Just a hint of the boy squinting into the sun from Aban's MySpace page.

"Make no mistake," warns Aida, "he is trained military, prone to violent outbursts, and under a great deal of pressure. I would advise you to make your presence known early on, so as not to spook him. His psychographic profiling indicates a strong moral compass, although he is impulsive. Make it obvious you are unarmed, untrained, no threat at all. He is not likely to hurt you unnecessarily." Aida's counsel fills me with self-doubt.

"Are you confident I'm equipped to talk someone like this down? I work in physics. I don't have any specialist training."

"I can't tell you how valuable you are to us, Sirona." Aida encourages earnestly. "No-one else in Taima would be able to arrange this type of unregulated port travel outside of the Dastband. It means the world."

"You can trust I won't sleep until I locate the trace on Tapuat. I can confirm it has Disengaged hidden within your Yasland apartment building, possibly underground. Though we have the man power to get it out unnoticed, I would not be willing to initiate Reengagement until we can confirm Waterson would be willing to cooperate." Kennen rationalises. It's a fair point. Aban, or Tapuat, has been through enough. There is no point switching it on again without Ben.

Aida finds my eyes. "If we can reunite this pair, there is hope for us all. It's just the beginning. Imagine the possibilities. Just try to keep your Igo in mind. Remember why you contacted us in the first place. You'll find your strength there."

10. "Rachel travailed in childbirth, and she had hard labor. Now it came to pass, when she was in hard labor, that the midwife said to her, "Do not fear; you will have this son also." And it was so, as her soul was in departing (for she died), that she called his name Ben-Oni; but his father called him Benjamin. But Jacob, because he would not renew the sorrowful remembrance of the mother's death every time he called his son by his name, changed his name, and called him Benjamin, the son of my right hand; that is, 'very dear to me, set on my right hand for a blessing, the support of my age, like the staff in my right hand.'" – Genesis 35:16-19

Although I have arrived past mid-afternoon to avoid midday sun, the soaring temperature is tangible on the other side of the port. It's a gush of warmth reminding me of the thrill of the Eco Dome opening for The Green Gala. A stretch of arta shrubs sprawl out in front of me, unrolling as far as I can see to the south-east, which look as though they have been cultivated to slow down the sand storm Shamal winds. There must be some kind of a base beyond, where Ben is camping. I remove my mask to take a swig of water and begin walking.

The shrubs are tall enough to cast shadows, darting and dancing onto the sand beneath. I had not wanted to take him by surprise, but my guess is that my approach is hidden in amongst this tall vegetation, so I am careful to make plenty of noise.

I hum the words to 'Bitter Sweet Symphony', suddenly grateful to Kennen for sourcing the comforting lyrics to the tune I heard Aban – or rather, Tapuat - play in my kitchen all those weeks ago, while the stalks spear their seeding barbs into my trouser hem. The sanded winds whip up back there, as I leave the dunes and flats behind me. My visor is still pulled low, to protect my eyes from the sand and sun, when I see a reflection bound after me.

I swing around, heightened, alert - and catch sight of an albino cape hare vaulting swiftly into the tall grasses.

As abruptly as I turned, I glimpse in my peripheral vision a large, dark implement swerving towards the left side of my head, connecting with a resounding crack, and reverberating through my skull. My knees give way from underneath me and the rest of my body drops. As my vision blurs and spins, I look up to see him looming over me, a tarpaulin hooding his head, with a thick, gnarled tree branch hanging from his right hand.

I don't know how many hours later it is when I wake up. It's cold and dark, leading me to question if I am still in the desert, given the low temperature. I'm in some type of underground chamber. I try to sit up, but my hands are tied flat to my waist.

"I gotta apologise, for all the ...precautions. I suffer from intrusive flashbacks. They make some of my behaviour hyper-vigilant." Ben has me hooked up to a Stem-Cellar powered by a portable generator. He opens the cryo-chamber and smears some of the serum across the side of my head. I blink through a haze. He looks older than the photo images Kennen provided in the brief. His skin is sun-scorched, and his matted hair is dishevelled. There is an echo still, of the skinny boy I saw on Tapuat's MySpace page. His tarpaulin cloak is discarded on the floor and I now notice he is still dressed in Scavak khaki.

"What is this place?" My voice is cracked and hoarse.

"I thought you'd be more comfortable under here, given that you're used to the Eco Dome. You're from the citadel, right?"

I gaze up to take in the vast structure, domed above and caved out below us. It is indeed cool.

"It's a Yakhchal, my Pa built it. These're pretty common across the gulf in Persia, in the Esfahani D'hasht. It's an evaporative cooler. See the qanat there? That's an aqueduct channelling water from the cooler north side. It's fed by the cold, collecting precipitation from the atmosphere. The dome above us is a badgir – a wind catching tower funnelling cooled air down, and the warm air up and out. I remember mixing up the sarooj mortar of sand and ash and goat hair every so often, and then watching the adults in the settlement using it to plaster the badgir. It's heat-resistant, you know. Ancient tech, but Ecologists know not to forget these things."

"Hey, I'm sorry about your head," he repeats. "Can't be too careful. You've got enough replacement serum for your regeneration wristband now."

"Why have you tied me up? I'm unarmed."

"You're a threat. I have to interrogate you to ascertain how much of a threat you are and who you've alerted."

I tell him I'm going to vomit and need to pee, so he cuts the ties from my ankles, and we move outside. It is getting darker. I am still tied up and cannot control the shuddering tremors in my limbs as he pulls my clothes off so I can pee. Until I'm covered up again, I am sure he is going to attack me.

Before long, Ben is basting a desert hedgehog over a fire on a spit and uses a make-shift metal box to roast turgid panic grass grains. He offers me some sort of brewed tincture. "It's just tea – Christ's thorn, desert hyacinth, Arabian gum," he assures me. "They're all medicinal, settle the stomach."

"You could untie me, instead of cup-feeding me tea." I point out.

"Why're you here?"

"To bring you back to Taima."

"Now, why would I go back? Look at the sunset."

Up around us, soar the wind-whipped, surrealist shapes of the sand fossils, gnarly and billowing, punctured with holes. The setting sun highlights the contrast in every textured ripple and crease, turning the fossils from shameless red, to spiced brown, to a deep, purple velvet, and at last soaking them an inky, saturated navy, in full drama against the burnt spilling ochre wash of the yellowing sky.

"I'm never going back. I belong here. Why would I trust you - a wandering stranger? Why would I trust anyone? I've no ties in Taima – they sold me back to the FIRE Centre rather than inconvenience themselves with my self- destruction." He is working himself into a frenzied rage. "The irony is that since I've been back at the Abani Lake I don't need their tranquilisers and sedatives forced down my throat. Or into my veins, or into my lungs! Troops reared on the trash! Who sent you?"

"Aida Socorro." I cower.

"Never heard of her."

"She kept records of children separated from domestic Igos at the border." I blurt out, instinctively curling into a ball.

"Then she's part of the problem. Who are you?"

"No! She wanted to reunite children to their Igos!" It takes all my efforts to collect my calm and speak coherently. I have to deescalate, not fuel the fire. I take a breath. "My name is Sirona Aeson. How can you expect a successful interrogation if your subject is too afraid of you losing your temper to answer honestly?"

"I don't expect honesty from anybody. My tendency to lash out is an issue for you, not for me."

"What if I told you Tapuat was looking for you all these years? What if I told you Tapuat is waiting for you back in Taima? It turned up at my door, recalibrated, but still searching for you. If you hadn't smashed up my visor, I could have shown you!"

"Tapuat wouldn't recognise what I've become! I've done things I don't wanna live with." Ben's eyes bulge and his voice is strangled. A vein throbs at his temple. "No one can be trusted, not you, not me! I became the same self-serving Scavak, numbed and drugged into raiding and rounding up Gedahi children from poisoned settlements, to traffic into the citadel! I don't deserve to hold those hands again!" He is incensed, screaming and spitting.

"Whose hands did Tapuat harvest? Are you a match? Those hands are so old – if only you could see them! Your Stem-Cellar could be a match. You could ease your Igo's suffering.

It doesn't care how you turned out! It just wants you back, Ben." I plead.

At this, his fury subsides, faintly. After a few moments, as calm ascends, Ben begins to answer.

"After the Sickness, Tapuat harvested the right hand of my Pa and the left hand of my Ma, so that I'd be comforted through the trek we'd have to endure across the D'hasht. Tapuat was sure it'd be safer for me inside the citadel, as my Pa had spent his whole life singing the praises of the noble Ethicists who were scientists just like us. So naïve - we didn't know then that it was Taima itself spraying the Sickness. Tapuat's hands carried four gallons of water and packed another 60 on camel-back. We got as far as the Albihoth ruins, when I got ill. We had to stop there so I could recover. I speculate in hindsight; it was simple dehydration. Tapuat caught lizards and Arabian spiny mice for me to eat. It taught me how to gut them and roast them as my parents had done, back at our settlement. Once Tapuat even killed a caracal cat, although I cried so much it never killed another cat again. I remember finally reaching the FIRE Centre solar walls, where the metal was so reflective it looked like the mirrors were built of sun itself. The walls radiated a heat so vicious that I didn't need Tapuat's warning not to get too close or touch them. That's when the Scavak surfaced from inside. They wrenched me from my Ma's hand. They didn't let us say goodbye. They Disengaged Tapuat right in front of me.

"I don't remember much immediately after that – I've problems with memory-lapses, flashbacks, guilt, numbness. You understand. Or maybe you don't. You can see I'm more than a little ... jumpy."

"They are not here anymore though, your family. You could catch the Sickness yourself out here, just like they did."

"The Sickness won't be back here."

"Don't be ridiculous, it's everywhere."

"Why're you so sure of everything Taima has told you? Haven't you heard enough already to doubt what you think you know?" The wrath in his voice is climbing a notch. "Do you honestly believe that those drones are dropping seeds alone, directly over Gedahi camps?"

"That is a nonsense conspiracy!" He is crazy. I am tied up in the desert by a deranged man. It is entirely possible he is a lost cause, and while I'm at his mercy, by default, so am I.

"It's not. I know I'm safe here until another wandering Gedahi camp try to set up nearby. Most of them know not to stay still too long or the drones will come for them. If a Shamal storm breaks, I've a week's supplies stored in the underground caves. The Scavak won't bother sending a whole drone for one lone nomad – or even two. In fact, they're used to losing personnel to the desert. Many of us die wandering around in the heat after going rogue with PTSD. They won't bother coming for you either."

"That is where you could be wrong." I look up to the darkening sky. From the direction of the Taima Dastband in the north-west, I discern the recognisable mosquito hover of the whirring drones suspended in flight and gliding towards us. Ben follows my gaze.

He flinches, startled, and jumps up as if on a spring. "Damn you! This is your fault – they think we're a *camp*! Oh, I'll take

63

you back to Taima alright – and throw you into a goddamn turbine!"

He hauls me up to my feet. "You've got to keep up!" he yells, as he drags me to a Humvee parked up, a few metres away. "We've got to get away from here before they reach Alwathbah," he mutters, as the Humvee rattles over rocks and dirt, hurtling us north-west towards the citadel.

11. At the Benjamin Gate, the captain in charge of the guards arrested him and said, "You have deserted us!" – Jeremiah 37.13

The drone fleet, buzz overhead like locusts, five minutes into our escape.

Ben notices me squinting into the windshield to the darkening sky. "The Humvee isn't a trigger; we can go unnoticed. The homing programming is sending them to the site of the 'camp' the Scavak have detected. Our problem isn't that the drones are gonna drop a load right on top of us. Our problem is that after the Shamal, the Sickness'll be blown all over the D'hasht."

A twisting, howling, whirlwind brews further south-east behind us, beyond the Alwathbah wetlands. It is a ferocious tornado of brown, approximately five miles tall, spinning in an undulating, inverted pyramid, malignant and pulsing at the horizon's edge.

"A twister moves faster than a Humvee. There's at least ten kilometres between us, but it'll close in by the time we reach the Alajban gate, carrying the contamination with it. Timing'll be tight, we gotta act fast when operating the gate to get inside safely." Even as he speaks, the throbbing whirlwind is gaining ground on us. The shrieking screech of gusts in the distance grow louder each minute. Ben instinctively accelerates, anxiously checking the rear-view screens.

"It's an almost impossible shot. If we are caught in the Shamal, we won't be able to leave the Humvee for a week, until the contamination subsides?"

"Sickness or no, the Shamal is enough to kill us even without the spread from the drones which just passed us."

"Why would Taima deliberately poison the D'hasht? The Gulf? This undermines all the work we have ever done."

"Taima doesn't like to share. And who's gonna stop Taima taking whatever it wants?"

The ominous Alajban solar walls rise up ahead of us, mirroring the littered, browning sky. Menacingly, the reflection parallels the pursuing demon, just metres away. The wind is a baleful banshee wail, as rocks begin pummelling our vehicle, denting the back with missiles, closing in around the sides.

We're close to the border, close enough to make a run for it. Ben exits the driver's side, sprinting around the vehicle to let me out, all the while debris blowing up around him. As he flings the passenger door open, the wind whips his feet up from under him - he is caught, both in the violent gusts of the Shamal, and the sinister vector of a turbine to the right of the Humvee. My hands are still tied with a rag, and in a millisecond of adrenaline-induced resourcefulness, I lean out to him, hooking my tied wrists over his head in a loop, effectively preventing him from being carried off into the turbine. I hoist him further inside the Humvee, scared I am going to snap his neck. He is in. Scrabbling over him, I yank the door shut.

"Oh my God, are you ok? Are you ok?" I pant through heaving breaths.

He sits up rubbing his neck, while fumbling in his pocket. He retrieves a small blade and cuts the rags tying my wrists. "Where you gonna run? Back into the D'hasht?" He looks sheepish.

"I just saved you!" I cry indignantly. The Humvee is no longer being pelted by rocks and debris from outside, although the desert is still growling malevolently. "Why is it hushing?"

"The eye of the twister. I didn't realise it was so close, we should've waited for it." He reaches into a compartment near the controls and pulls out two protective oxygen masks. "Put it on. No way of knowing how much contamination has already carried this far."

The Shamal ebbs suspiciously, as Ben continues. "Stay away from turbines – as you've seen, the vacuum is enough to get an arm or leg caught if a gust of wind pushes you near. Stay away from the solar walls. Even in the lower evening temperatures they retain enough heat to burn your skin off through your clothes. The eye will allow us a few moments to run, and for me to wave my prints over the entry scanner at the gate. Do you follow?"

I nod.

Outside the Humvee, the quiet is eerie as a hunt, the soupy air a thickening predator. It's our only chance to dart across the ten or so metres between the Humvee and the gate, fighting the snarl and suck of the turbine to the right of us. As we approach the gate, a blur of stalking sands bluster at our backs, already threatening to devour us.

Ben is losing it. His waving hand frantically, repetitively, swipes past the prints scanner. "Damn it! They've deregistered my prints as 'missing in action'!" he spits through gritted teeth.

"They wouldn't lock you out. They know you are still alive!"

"They would."

The door slides open abruptly with a clunk, just as the squall catches up. Tempest sands hound in after us, as we tumble on to the concrete floor of the Dastband. Ben struggles up to standing and slams the seal button. The door clanks shut, bolting the storm firmly outside.

"We're in the decontamination tank." He explains, as he notices me looking around. "Put on the goggles. It's UV in there, it'll burn your skin like hell but not as much as the Sickness would. Nothing a Stem-Cellar can't sooth afterwards. The jets'll hose you down. Put your clothes in the incinerator, there'll be khaki at the other end. You have to run through on the treadmill and breathe deep – the exercise forces the nebulised agent further into your lungs and blood stream."

I follow Ben's instructions through the UV tank. The Scavak khaki is too big for me, and my skin is smarting, but I'm glad to be clean and dry. To my surprise, when I exit the tank, Troy appears before me, stepping through a port.

"Troy! I can't tell you how glad I am to see you! How did you know where to look for me? I thought you didn't want to get involved?" I pull him in for a hug, grinning from ear to ear, laughing with relief.

"I detected you destroyed one of my visors, and your chip reading recorded you had been asleep for eighteen hours! So, I contacted Kennen. I had a feeling he was mixed up in this. He told me you were busy testing portals outside the Alajban border using a temporary chip. Well, then I knew you were in deep – implanting a temporary chip! Honestly, Sirona, have you lost your mind? Against my better judgement, I've been jumping back and forth to this tank all day, hoping you'd materialise sooner or later. You had me worried there, with the storm looming. Who's that behind you?"

"That's Ben Waterson, a Scavak who brought me back inside. We got caught in the Shamal. He's... er, jittery. Don't startle him." I advise Troy. "Can you get us to my apartment without us having to go through the border controls?"

"Your apartment?"

"Yes. Did you bring any visors?"

"Thought you could do with a few spares. What about your friend?"

"His chip is Scavak issue, they already know where he is. Nobody seems to care. He was AWOL, registered 'missing in action'."

Ben emerges from the tank.

"Who're you?" Ben grunts, as ever, immediately guarded and defensive.

"It's alright, this is my colleague, Troy. Troy, meet Ben. Troy will get us out, untraced. Once we're cleaned up, we can regroup with Kennen and Aida. They need to know about the drones."

"OK," Ben agrees decisively. "Let's get out of here."

12. "Christianity is not about the divine becoming human so much as it is about the human becoming divine. That is a paradigm shift of the first order." - John Shelby Spong.

"You know, Troy, I'm so very sorry to get you mixed up in all of this." I say as we port into my apartment. "But I am so glad you turned up just when we needed you."

"Mixed up in what?" he chortles. "There's no possible trace on those anonymous chips and visors, the authorities have no clue your Igo malfunctioned, and no interest in Ben's whereabouts. We've spent every lunchtime together for six years, so I don't think anyone will find it out of the ordinary that I've been to your apartment. If I'm asked about Ben being here too, it's nothing they don't already know. Don't worry about people stealing your ideas. If your ideas are any good you will have to ram it down their throats to get them to pay attention. You haven't got me mixed up in anything, no need to worry."

"And yet…" I prompt him.

"…You know I could be a help to you? I know there's more going on than just trying to find a match for that Igo's hands."

"Once you know what I know, you can't un-know. You don't want to carry this, believe me. I guarantee I'll call you in some desperate fix before long anyway – or you'll surprise me by showing up in your figurative armour again!" I try to make light of it, like we used to when things were pressurised at the University. It makes me feel better for a little while, laughing with a friend together like this. But there's a lump in my throat

71

which will not swallow away. One day I'll repay him his kindness.

"Did I hear someone offer some help?" Aida calls from my sitting room. She and Kennen arrived sometime before us, and have brought Tapuat up here, from the basements below my apartment building where it was hiding. The Igo is completely still and rigid in its temporary rigor mortis. It makes me shudder. A battle of hope and sadness in equal measure.

"Give me an underground research facility, half a dozen molecule-smashers, a beautiful alien in a diaphanous veil waiting to be turned into a rhesus monkey, and I care not who writes the Cyrus Cylinder declaration of universal rights." Troy jokes and extends his hand to Aida. "Good to meet you, I'm Troy." He concludes, as Aida returns his greeting.

"You sound like a man after my own heart," quips Kennen.

"Dr Shepherd." Troy nods cordially.

"Troy, is it? Another alumni of mine, no doubt? Good, good, marvellous to know the University keeps you all so busy once you are out of my lecture halls. Very well then, your first task is to help me carry up the Stem Cellar from Aida's Humvee parked two blocks from here."

Aida waves them off as I set about reactivating my own chip. I have been officially 'sleeping' for too long, suspiciously enough for Troy to question it. If anybody else decided to dig around they would be sure to notice that much.

Ben watches on with interested disgust from the doorway. I stand at my bathroom mirror and use a penknife to make an incision at my temple, just as Kennen taught me. A trickle of blood instantly drips from the site as I squeeze out the anonymised chip like a blackhead. It lands in the porcelain basin below with a tinkle. I swap it for my own chip, which I scoop out of its resting place - my supply of serum from my Stem-Cellar. Wincing, I push my own chip into the cut as far as it will go, holding the tear together as the serum seals the wound.

"Hhmmm. Didn't think you had that in you." Ben observes. His focus shifts to the sitting room where the Igo stands, tomb-still. His eyes are set on Tapuat, as I watch his expression change to bewilderment, then anguish. At Tapuat's side now he sits, his hands covering his face, his shoulders curled into his stomach. "Where's the Stem Cellar already?" he sobs softly.

"On the way." says Aida. "They can't port it up here, it's too big. They have to use the elevator." It remains unspoken between us that there is no guarantee Tapuat will Reengage.

"With Troy otherwise occupied, we have an opportunity to fill in some gaps." she continues. "You know Ben, you are the first child to find your domestic Igo. We will need Tapuat's help too of course, the connections it made with other Igos using Perl and MySpace incognito. You could lead us to help many more separated children find the last of their family."

"There's more Aida, it's so much worse than we could have imagined – what Taima is doing out there! Ben – tell her about the drones, tell her what they're doing." I urge him.

Troy and Kennen arrive with the Stem-Cellar, shortly after Ben has explained the Spray-drones' primary function is to drop the Sickness onto Gedahis. Ben is already almost asleep

73

as we connect him to the Stem-Cellar. The garnering process saps the last of his energy for the night.

I see Troy, Kennen, and Aida to the door. As Kennen and Troy port through, I ask Aida, "Are you coming back tomorrow?"

"No need to."

"But don't you want to see them together?" I had expected her to look happier. After all, her decades-long efforts have finally come to fruition.

But Aida's face is graveyard-pale. "We have done all we can here. But there's more outside. Ben has told us that there is a deliberate flow of terrorised children to the FIRE Centre. It's beyond anything plausible we could have guessed. There is no end to the self-interest! And to hell with their Cyrus Cylinder declaration of universal rights. That is where our focus must move now. I'll leave Ben and Tapuat to their private celebrations – or consolations – tomorrow. We have so much work to do. I will be in touch." She disappears with the portal swishing shut behind her.

13. "Tapuat: A symbolic emblem of concentric circles forming a maze leading to a spot at the centre. Connoting: a) the mother/ child dyad. b) the cycle of life. c) the spirit returning to its source. d) the umbilical cord. e) humanity's connection to the mother, earth, and cosmos. F) an initiative map to higher understanding." Native North American Hopi tribe

We wait for night, so Tapuat can see the moon if Reengagement goes well. Today is June 21st, 2130, summer solstice. It is a beautiful full moon for Tapuat.

Kennen is setting up equipment to begin Reengagement. "Be prepared for disorientation," he warns us, guardedly. "Igos are often confused, subdued after Reengagement as they get their bearings. We must factor in too, that a recalibrated Igo has already been subjected to years of nanotabak onslaught. Give it some time, don't expect an immediate reaction."

Ben is quiet. He wrings his hands, paces, broods. "Even if it wakes up, how do we protect it now? No one even believes it deserves any help."

I don't know what to say. "It could stay here? You know I will look after it. You can visit anytime."

"You're busy, at the University, and with all of …this. I can't see you stopping now. I've time, now that the Scavak have changed my status to 'rehabilitation following trauma'. It seems like Aida wants you on board too. Once this blows over, I guess she could use me too, huh? Like an insider?"

"You'll have to take it home with you then. I can sign the ownership documents over. I only bought it to cover for my own while it's repaired. You don't need to report the malfunction, do you?"

He nods, relieved. "I'll always be indebted to Aida. She's the first to care what happened to those kids, you know. But Sirona, you're the first human to care enough to help an Igo, just for the Igo's sake, not a human's. Aida cares for human children and human futures, but you cared for the Igo. My selfless, invisible, indispensable Igo."

"Without whose surrogacy we are all doomed. Aida taught me that."

"Science can never solve one problem without creating ten more. Computer science is less about computers than astronomy is about telescopes. Shall we begin?" Kennen suggests gently. "All set."

The process is unceremonious. Routers and wires are connected, then a simple flick of a switch. The anti-climax is intolerable. Tapuat is obviously switched on but shows no movement. The defeat is crushing. The weight of it unbearable.

"Tapuat, can you hear me? It's me, Benjamin. I found you. I'm with you. I'm with you." He clutches Tapuat's hands, massages the serum into the arthritis. At once the liver spots rub away, creases disappear and wrinkles smooth. "That's it, my love. I'm back to care for you now. We're together." He bends to kiss Tapuat's left knuckles. And the Igo, with a barely discernible movement, achieves a tiny, deliberate, responsive squeeze of his hand.

THE LEGEND OF BAGULEY BROOK

Onst upon a time, long, long ago, in The Land of the Brooks, in deepest Cheshire, lived a woodcutting family. Seven brothers lived there on a shielded quillet of lowe-land by Baguley Brook, in a stronghold of a cottage with their Oma, that is to say, their mother's mother. Oma had lost her only daughter seven Springtimes gone, through a fever, after the poor wench birthed Oma's youngest grandson. Shortly after, Oma's son-in-law followed, afflicted by a broken heart. Fortunately for the new infant, Oma was also the local Cunning Woman, and so was well versed in when, and under which moon, to harvest the particularest herbs and roots, from the fens, and pewit wet-flats, to pummel and brew into tinctures to be taken as tea. She had midwifed nearly all the local children, and oft tended to a stung knee with a kiss and a thrice-chant of "Dock come in, Nettle go out." It was thus the infant survived, as Oma was able to wet-nurse him hersell, in spite of her ancient fragility and rheumatiz. Many a neighbour, on seeing the boy, exclaimed: "He's doesom, for lack of diddy," as he thrived into fine fettle, despite his absent mother.

The seventh brother came to be known as the Hatchling, on account of his motherless state, and his golden downy halo of hair, making him appear much akin to the chicks hatched the Easter after his birth.

The family lived in easy comfort with six fligge-fledged grown men who put grout afore brass. The House Place floor Oma swept by broom each evening was oak rather than earthen. The skreen by the fireplace, and squab-sofa, were carved delicately and ornately from fine timber, by the most artistic brother, who was in truth, more of a sculptor than a Hatchet. To each brother a Kibbo-Kift, a gift of skill; Axeman, Feller, Hatchet, Joiner, Brancher, Sawgate – and all six were accomplished carpenters. On mearh-back each

morning, they would load their snap-tins full of Oma's pikelet cakes, to ride dobbin carts into the holt woodlands beyond the Plain Road. Each morning the Hatchling would help Oma with lithing the porridge in the kilner afore it cruddled, whilst begging to take his place as Snagghand amongst his brothers.
"Tha's still of no mickles!" the eldest would retort.
"The scranny lad's too lile!" agreed the next.
"Three more summers are to wither afore tha joins 'em, Hatchling. Tha's still an Atchen, but soon to be Oak." decreed Oma. One morning, the boy looked so forlorn in the face, that the talented sculptor threw the Hatchling a toy swordfish carved from wood, from the departing cart, by way of condolence.

Each evening the six brothers would return - onmost clem-starved - to the cottage where Oma's tatty cakes and Fitchet pie filled the House Place with the sticky warmth of lobscouse, bacon and apple. Soon, the eight of them would be sipping Oma's distilled Geneva Plums, essole-rooting together around the fire's orange flicker of kindlestuff. Each brother would boast that it was he, who had been the most o'er-mowed with treowfellin', going giddy on mead over which gallas young fellow had been the regular gad-about that day, or who had blushed the most at the reet-pommer dairymaids. What a rabblement of rakussing was made! Until Oma cried "Me head's all of a missock!"

"Now childer! Oil have no overs left, by leddy!" as she pointed to the red pan-mugs, piled with food on the sturdy table. "Art 'oo clem-starved, or ney?"
A great rush then ensued in making for the table, shocking Oma's poor familiar kyat to cease licking its paws and instead bolt in fright.

And so, The Hatchling lived in the insulated shade of this assured fortress, spending his youngest days in safe hylet with his Oma to himself.

***

"But why Oma? I wunnu stay essole-rooting wi' t'others!" The Hatchling would protest at bedtime.

"A loaze for meddlers! Enough of your gammock, now to bed." Oma would reply.

In bed, and under his hilling-blanket, he neezled cosily to Oma's bossom. "He's none sleeping, he's only foxin'" she would whisper affectionately, as she neshined his sweet golden head and feathery eyebrows.

"Tell me a nomony Tall-Tale, Oma. A Smuggler's Tale," he asked. In recent nights, Oma had with some trepidation - given the Hatchling's tender age - recounted terrifying Old Maritime stories, passed along the hidden Wallasey tunnels and taverns along the Mersey's riverbanks. Still, the boy's morbid fascination with such ordeals led him to beg her each night for another. Even as Oma cushioned her Hatchling in an embrace, she could not avoid the foreboding she felt so acutely with each night's request. The child was gorby-soft with sweetness, and so with angst and misgiving, she began her yarn.

"The Fremfolk sailors who traverse the Great Orme, regaled accounts of an owd submerged church bell, tolling out a cloudy disturbance from under the sea. It travelled to the coasts of North Wales, recited in the alehouses of the Hoylake Beaches and the mizzled banks of the Mersey, till it trickled along the eye of our own Baguley Brook… the Tale of Owd Peg Powler."

"Oma, oo's Peg Powler?" the Hatchling asked, and Oma dreaded his innocent calfish-gurr, knowing he would be most affeared of the monster. Still, it would keep him on the safer hassock-grasses and away from the moiling mizmaze of the water's rundle-edge, where he was prone to absent-mindedly loppen.

"Why, she's my own Bete Noire, lad." Oma replied. Then she sang sweet and low, a song of an old adversary, who had made to snatch each of her grandsons at least once during their loumest years.

"Peg is Gefion's merewif,
dividing land and sea.
She's Grendel's vengeful Modor:
Ides, the Valkyrie.

Peg Powler, High Green Ghostess,
with crown of tresses green.
Her ribboned reeds, and lacing weeds,
are manacles, unseen.

With skin of frog and fingers webbed,
she rides a log, half-sunk.
Her skin's disguised in garments,
sewn of algae and gunk.

Peg tangles wading ankles
from shallows to the deep,
her Ginny Greenteeth dragging catches
silently to sleep.

The surface scum is Old Peg's Cream,
to warn of the Child-Drowner.
You'll know her by the water's froth,
the Suds of Old Peg Powler"

"Lawk, how oi've skeered oo, my nursle lad," she murmured as she saw the tremble in his cheek, and hesitated a haffle, as she held him tight. Oma was most overcome hersell, by the bitter-sweet terry-devil of love's unease. So, she kickled his ribs till he laughed out rutes of pure joy, and planted mickle kisses on every peckle-freckle, remembering rightly, that his kisses were her best endurance against the frosts. They were Blestian, after all.

"But is she real, Oma?" the boy persisted.

"Callin' me a ligger, lad? Reports are ryfe, folk does sen so many a time an' oft… Oi heard tell from a Murenger-Officer from Ceazester misell," qualmed Oma.

"Tis certain so, till Ridley Pool be mown and sown, or Redesmere Lake floats once more! Here, hold your carved swordfish. Folk sen the swordfish is Peg's familiar. With thine dannies full, there'll be no room for mischief n' tice near the bullyed tadpoles tomorrow, the onliest place where she'd be lurkin."

With the Hatchling and Oma satisfied for safety, she re-joined her six older grandsons around the House Place hearth, until at last, the cottage went quiet, and nowt could be heard but the hillhooting owls and the babbling of Baguley Brook.

***

82

It was the Hatchling's seventh Spring, not long after the Pace Eggs had been painted, and the buzzing waps fetched in the new season's heat. The Hatchling was stringing his gled-kite and making a mither of himsell.

"Tha's made a muxt on it, lad." This warm aundernoon, Oma was in no mood for tantrels.

"I've summat for you to back your teeth to," Oma offered the Hatchling. "Past the shippen shed, the fruit is all over-mosey already. You're a dab hand at scrumping so you are! Oi seen ye eating those Hawthorn shoots like Bread 'n Cheese all morn. Besides, you're rawnge under me feet indoors. Hie haste, afore it fares o'raining."

The Hatchling thought the chances of rain were laughable, but he knew better than to argue as he pulled on his wood-moggin clogs and stuffed a hitchen of bread in his pocket for the digg-ducks.

"Stay away from that there mere!" Oma called after him. "Beyond the meadow's a slutchy, mizzicky hole, full of sluther and nowt else!" She watched him with tense presentiment from the door as the Alder tree outside rustled with roosting Queeze pigeons. Oma had always shuddered at their nests, built so vulnerably that the eggs could be seen through the tree's branches.

The Hatchling daddled and dondered lythly, between the yellow daffadowndillies and violet moondaisies towards the cowshed. He hid there, laying down in the cool long green, to the twitter of the jacknickers, madgepies and jennywren. The mayflowers and bluebells bobbed their brazen indigos to dickiebird pipes and flutes, the white bloom of Lady's Smock kirtle-twirled and Faeries Petticotes on foxgloves danced, most pleasurable to look on, till the Hatchling fell to rest. Every now and again, a twinkle of sunbeam would flicker through the dappled shadows of Popilary leaves. He would open a sleepy eye to this Volta, a wash of scarlet from the tree's red-rag catkins emblazoned against the sapphire azure of the midday sky, the fuscia-stipple of Peter-Cowslips and blushing suffuse of nippernail-rosehips, or a sun-lemon dauble of marygoldings. The Robin Hood Breeze smelled as sugar-laiden as Oma's wild cherry pies.

The delicious scent reminded the Hatchling he had work to attend, and sluggishly he arose from the forget-me-nots and paigle primroses, with his basket, ready to collect gooseberries, San Jan pears, and Jacob's plums. For good measure, he picked Oma the bonniest piannot-peony in the quillet and added the poppies Oma used to make Pape's Milk, ample payment for the half of the harvest he had already eaten.

Then he remembered the hitchen of bread he had saved to throw for the diggs and their ducklings. The Hatchling looked back towards the cottage and saw Oma sitting shaded under hylet, darning a hilling blanket. She was unwatching. Hatchling put his basket down and disappeared behind the shippen shed, over the quillet boundary stones, toward the Palm Willow's feathery yellow blossoms, soft as goslings, hung low as a noose, over the water's cackling edge.

***

The water glistened in the bright light. The sparkles and pink grass beckoned the Hatchling, as he followed a shimmering edther-bart, its green and purple dragon skin an iridescent rainbow. Hatchling darted in between the prickers on the brimble, and the whabbock puddles to reach the spot most favoured by the diggs, although as yet, there were no diggs to be seen. Instead, like a gamol-ghast, a longnix heron, was stillness in the gurgling shallows, waiting for a penk-minnow or jacksharp to venture close enough to seize. The Hatchling wondered if it would steal the diggs' bread instead.

The Hatchling reached into his pocket and felt for the cob. It was crusty and tough in his fingers. Without looking, he threw the first pocketful out to the peck. As it arched a curve towards the burbling surface, the Hatchling saw that it was not bread he had thrown, but the carved swordfish his brother had gifted him. The longnix was disturbed. Razzored, it lifted away, leaving behind a curious skew-wifter of disturbance in the water. A misshapen scaum of cloud and scurry, eddied, peecing and rippling through the reeds. The percolation fizzed and bubbled to quiet, but the Hatchling was mouth-mud determined to see the cause, and in any case, he needed to retrieve his swordfish or there would be questions.

Gingerley, the Hatchling found footing onto the sniddlegrass, near an owd rampicked tree. The ground was a slathery slatter of moiling slop. He sken-squinted his eyes ill enough to pierce the watery glass and thought he may have seen either a sparling or his swordfish. He would need to wallow a little further, for the form of it to become clear from beneath the glinting reflective flashes on the surface.

Without nary a skroik of surprise, the boy's next nookshotten, ill-judged step, slid him overwelt and overwaiste, and with a heavy soss fell past the shallows. The entangling weeds clutched for him, and he was left rawing and pulling hissell from the nets to no avail, as the brook replaced the air in his lungs, silently.

***

From the hylet, a faint splash pungered Oma's old ears, followed by quank-quiet.

"Has the lad taken to napping, as moss caught in the mere again?" she mumbled to herself as she sewed. "Odd rabbit it!" she complained, as she rose her agged body from her rocking chair. Latafoot, and slow to move, on account of her obshackled knees, Oma felt weak and wammocky out in the sunshine away from her hylet. "Hatchling?" she cried "Hatchling, where be ye?"

"What the ferrups is he doing?" she chundered to herself, a distinct sense encroaching like winter fog, that her cherished boy was welly-marred. "Hatchling! Hatchling!"

Her breath wherked most feebly by the time she reached the rampicked tree, and her heart a madpash of terror. The water had her sibbed-kin in a giant's hold underneath itself, and floating as wood ought, a carved swordfish returned upon the surface.

THE FLEDGLING HEART

The Fledgling Heart

Tuesday 6th November 2018

It was early hours, when my heart fell out. I had taken myself off to bed at around seven, feeling a trifle off colour, but not suspecting anything so serious.

Quietly, so as not to wake Paul, I crept downstairs. As I rummaged around in the back of the fridge, hunting for some Gaviscon, a burning line, seared vertically, somewhere between my navel and my chin. I tore open my nightshirt, as to my horror a deep, red, welted streak appeared, like an ugly, slug-like stretch mark, and rapidly began to split into a tear.

It's so beyond what I can begin to understand, I'm going to try to write it out. Maybe it will stop me from going mad.

Honestly, looking back, I couldn't say now whether I actually heard a rip, or if this is my mind's attempt to embody the pain. A jarring, gruff, unexpected rupture. Oh, it was bitter, to the sound of a pair of jeans ripped in January after too many mince pies.

Underneath my cracking ribs pulsed a thunder. The thudding of it shook my whole torso, building in tempo, until finally my heart burst forth from the gash in my chest and performed a bouncing commando roll onto the kitchen tiles five feet away.

It made quite a grisly mess; I can tell you. Incredibly, my first thought was how I could hope to clean it all up. Then my full attention turned to the pitiful thing, and - hand on heart (if I still had one) - I can truthfully swear, that is where my full attention has been ever since. It was gory and pulsing, its tender meats exposed to germs and cold. Veins and tentacles flayed around distressingly, searching out the nervous system which had only just ejected it. Instinctively, I rushed to my heart and scooped the thing up, but beyond instinct I'm not sure what I was doing at all. The fact that I had survived an injury that should have killed me, had not yet dawned on me.

As if the morning's event were not unusual enough, my heart then began to behave of its own accord. From its largest arteries at the top, formed a mouth-like organ, which began stretching towards me, rooting and searching. I watched, revolted, mesmerised, and utterly riveted to the spectacle. The mouth sought gently and with purpose until it located a protruding blueish vein between my shoulder and my neck, where it fastened itself and executed on me, what I can only describe as a hiccie. Very soon after, my heart relaxed to a calm stillness, and an exhausted relief weighed heavily upon us both. We remained there, on the kitchen floor with the fridge door still open, until Paul found us at breakfast.

"Oh my God, Becky!" he exclaimed predictably, as you would. "Can you speak? I must call an ambulance! What happened?"

"My heart, it just ... jumped right out. But look, it's reattached itself, sort of."

"It '*jumped* out'? What do you mean? How are you still breathing?!"

Neither of us could make sense of the night's proceedings. However, after some superficial discussion, we decided perhaps it was best not to seek medical attention. Once Paul pointed out that I am a medical marvel, inexplicable by modern science, I became fearful that I would be subject to all kinds of research and most likely, permanently separated from my heart – a notion I could not begin to fathom without sickening panic. Besides, who would believe me anyway?

The noise of our discussion had disturbed its leeching from my jugular, and my heart briefly disengaged itself. I took this small respite, as an opportunity to inspect the damage to my chest. Astoundingly, the wound had already crusted over and begun to heal, although the horror on Paul's face at the sight of the wound would not suggest such a thing.

"Oh, it was a lot worse an hour ago. It's already plugging up." I reassured him.

I had only put it down for a moment, but the terror of our separation seemed to creep into my heart's awareness too. Home is where the heart is, and my heart was homesick. The mouth it had grown for blood-letting, began to bleat a soul-curdling scream, bursting with woe and desperation. My entire being shook with pity and every cell in me felt the urge to reconnect to and comfort my poor, pathetic heart. Immediately, I scooped up my heart and held it close to the vein so that it might find solace and stability there. I wondered if my heart would ever allow me to get up off the kitchen floor.

Paul watched on, entirely stupefied and aghast at the screaming bloodbath before him.

"I'm going to need a lot of your help. I don't think it will let me move."

Monday 12ᵗʰ November 2018

Over the week, me and my heart have managed to get into a sort of rhythm. Our greatest difficulty is when I have a task other than blood-letting to perform, like cooking a risotto for example. Suffice to say, the risotto, and all other focus-demanding tasks are hitherto and swiftly abandoned for the foreseeable. During one snatched shower time, I had to allow my heart to continue its relentless leaching while I soaped my hair. The shrieking was simply unbearable, and not a consequence worth enduring. I have no strategies on how I'm to go back to work once my impromptu holiday leave expires.

"You can't keep dropping everything every time it screeches. How can you carry on like that?" Paul asked me irritably today. No sleep is taking its toll. Although I've tried to keep it in a drawer at night for Paul's sake, the wretched thing was so loud and high pitched there was no sleeping through it. The drawer solution (which is proving to be no solution at all) was my way of putting Paul first. But there was a cost to me, and to my heart. Worse than the torture of no sleep, was a gut-twisting panic about *missing* this important siren, which felt like an abhorrent betrayal to myself and my pitiful screaming heart. Paul didn't share this perspective.

Inevitably, I've realised the only way either of us might ever sleep again, is to give in and facilitate my heart's uninterrupted access to my blood supply. I've taken to sleeping sitting up on the armchair downstairs rather than risk waking Paul up. At least he isn't disturbed, and my heart only shrieks momentarily as I can keep it close. It is only me who is left exhausted, but I figure this is all my own fault for not agreeing to Paul's suggestion of locking it in the bathroom while we sleep or attempt to.

Wednesday 21st November 2018

Paul is trying to be supportive.

"It's called The Plasmatic 2000. Look." Paul beamed this afternoon, thrusting his phone under my nose. He is fearful about how we will survive on only one wage if I don't go back to work next week.

"You fill it with blood, and it'll spray down your heart to keep it quiet," he explained helpfully. "See here, the review says, 'The Plasmatic 2000 takes care of your 'Fledging Heart' so you can continue your other daily tasks uninterrupted.'"

"What's 'Fledgling Heart'? Let me see." It sounded too good to be true. There must be a catch.

Simply set the timers and fill The Plasmatic 2000 with pig blood, readily available from most high street butchers, sit back and let The Plasmatic 2000 do the rest! The Plasmatic 2000 can accommodate up to 16 hours of continuous blood supply for survivors of Fledgling Heart. At last, you can carry on with the life you're used to leading and forget about your heart!

"I'm not leaving my heart alone without me for sixteen hours, getting sprayed down with disgusting pig's blood, by a machine! Are you insane?" This is probably the most merciless and repellent thing I have ever seen on the internet. I couldn't really convey this to Paul who thinks it is the answer to all our problems.

Although the existence of a market for such a repugnant device exists is in itself tragic and abysmal, one good thing about the barbaric pig-blood-sprayer-device is that it was my catalyst into some web-based rabbit holes, where I quickly learned I was not alone. I detest the internet, so I couldn't bear too much research on Fledgling Hearts before I resorted to calling my media filter, Magda.

Thursday 22nd November 2018

"Oh yeah, it's one of those conditions, you know, like ME and POTs and Fibromyalgia, and all those. Loads of support groups on social media platforms and stuff. Except FH is more Sigourney Weaver if you know what I mean. Obvious gore."

"What do you mean? What's 'one of those conditions' mean?"

"Like, the people who suffer hardly ever get believed and they get constant bad advice that even makes them worse sometimes. There's all sorts of fuss on one of the Twitter feeds recently – can't remember which disease, it's one that makes you really tired – anyway, some so-called-experts told them to exercise - when actually they should rest - and made them all even sicker!" As usual, Magda drew almost no breath to spill out her font.

"Why wouldn't anyone believe that my heart's jumped out? They can see it!" The evidence was damning after all. Anyone can see and hear it for themselves. In fact, they would have no choice about that.

"I dunno. Classic gaslighting probably. Just keep ignoring and deflecting what the sufferer says they're experiencing, hoping they'll go away and be quiet. The Fledgling Heart threads are having a controversy about the *cold* right now." Magda lives for internet injustice and conspiracy, although her insight here seems alarmingly prophetic. I hadn't gone to my GP or called an ambulance because I really couldn't grasp how anyone else would even believe it. Of course, that was before I knew it was a *thing*.

"Oh yeah, I read that too. Sounds counter-intuitive to me. I know my heart needs to be near me because I'm warm and it knows it's safe. It screams like hell when it gets cold, and it starts to look grey and sick," I added, rather proud of my novice research. I don't often have an opinion on internet debates, but this one riled me. I do not want to be separated from any of my organs. It seemed third parties were pushing for longer separations of hearts from bodies and were deliberately misdirecting the cruelty of refrigeration as some sort of health benefit, necessary for commerce and the economy. The Fledgling Heart sufferers who are desperate to earn a crust cling to it, most likely because it eases the contrition of their cognitive dissonance, being forced to reject their own hearts day in day out.

"Anyway, I know that what happened to you also happened to Denise Price from Accounts, when she was younger. She used to put her heart in one of the lockers. But it stopped screaming years ago, so now she just leaves it there all night too, to get some peace at home. It's actually very common. I bet loads of people have been through it and we don't know." Magda's gossiping was void of feeling, but it made me shudder.

"How could she *do* that? Her poor heart, giving up on her like that! It needed her; didn't she need it too? Abandoned in a locker at work! No wonder she is so dreary and sour... how on earth has her heart survived with so little blood?" It certainly explains a lot about Denise, who is on a spectrum somewhere between Teresa May and The Walking Dead.

"Well, there's not much else she could do, was there? God, don't be so judgmental, Becky! What are *you* going to do on Monday? You don't think Barbara the Borg is gonna let you deafen and douse the whole office, do you? And there'll be blood everywhere!"

Magda had a fair point. Her manner quietened, and after a pause, she took a tone of divulgence. "Do you remember last year when I found that lump in my breast? My hospital scan ran over. I rang Barbara to say I was held up waiting for my turn and she hung up on me… honestly Becks, I was more scared about the bollocking I was in for than I was about what the docs would find from the scan."

"Oh, I'm so sorry, Mags. What an odious bully. What happened?"

"You know, it came back normal after a few weeks. You remember."

"No, I know that! … I mean, what did Barbara the Borg do to you?"

"Yeah, she was vile. I was meant to get back at two, but it was near to three. Proper tore me a new one, even though I let her know. Shoulda finished at five that day but she said I had to stay till eight. Told Denise and the others I had taken the piss out of them for coming back late. Made me do all the really crap jobs no one would take on for weeks. Gave my desk to an intern while I was at a funeral. Kept butting in when I was in Strategy meetings in front of clients to cut me off. Tons of bad stuff. If I was you, I wouldn't even bother telling her. She'll pretend to care but the minute you hit a hurdle she'll be a toad about it." Deep breath Magda, deep breath. She had worked herself up and tears creaked behind her voice.

"I'm so furious for you, Mags. How come you never told me before?" God, I hate Barbara.

"Dunno, embarrassed, I guess. You know, when it came back fine after all. A storm in a teacup. Just wanted to ignore it till it went away. I was pretty miserable while I waited for the results though, and afterwards… when The Borg wouldn't let up. Anyway, I didn't want it to happen to you too." Magda sniffed.

"Thank you, hon." I appreciated her drudging up her brush with the intimidation tactics rife amongst our office overlords. "I wish you'd said. I mean, I know you told me about the lump, but about Barbara too."

I could hear her shrugging down the phone. "…So, what will you do? Doesn't sound like you're going to put it in a locker like Denise."

"Not a chance. It's ridiculous to expect people to live without their hearts. AND it's ridiculous of Barbara if she thinks I'm giving up work. There's no rule about hiding your heart in a locker before you can do your job. I'm just going to turn up and do my thing, heart and all. I'm just going to DO Monday. It's not against the law to walk around with your own vital organs intact."

"Hmmm. She'll make your life unbearable. It's called 'managing out dissent'. She's a control freak. And besides, what about the noise… and the mess? I'd definitely email her over the weekend if you're going to go through with it. A least she can't say you've sprung it on her."

"If I need extra time to clean up the mess, I'll ask for it. It's not unreasonable. As for the noise, my heart is calm enough so long as it's near me, or on me. It's only if I neglect it that it starts kicking up a stink."

"Ooooh we should get the girls in on this! I'll start a WhatsApp!" Magda enthused. And just like that, my keyboard crusader began typing out our rallying cry for a call to arms…

Friday 23rd November 2018

[Magda] *Has anyone got a heart they keep at home? What do you do with it all day while you're out?*

[Suneeta] *I don't, but Hardeep puts his in the fridge at his pharmacy. I think the cold helps it keep fresh and it's quieter in the evenings. They seem ok with it now, but the first few weeks was tough on them both.*

[Hayleigh] *Mine almost died one day when I left it too long!* (crying emoji*) I felt so sick and guilty!* (more emojis) *Now I keep it in the car in a cool box, so no-one is bothered by the noise between top ups. Cold def helps with the noise. They need the cold.*

[Suneeta] (broken heart gif)

[Me] *I had no idea you had both gone through this too. I'm going to try to bring mine into work on Monday, see if I can keep it bandaged up next to me.*

[Hayleigh] *What about The Borg? Can you cope with work without it getting in the way? Mine's so draining! I think maybe my heart would annoy me too much lolz* (laughing emoji) *plus how will u keep it cold?*

[Magda] *Anyone fancy a pizza night at mine tomorrow? Hearts welcome xxx*

Saturday 24th November 2018

The pizza night was very exciting. Magda's grip on all things viral really is a marvel. She decided she would bake ten artisan, vegan, sourdough pizzas. Apparently, the hashtags make her efforts worth it and sends our plans for Monday farther. "Wear something nice for the photos. You're the face of FH now," she warned me on Friday.

One by one the comrades buzzed the door to Magda's apartment.

"I brought you a present," gushed Claire, as she unwrapped a piece of colourful knotted silk, holding the corner apart and flapping out the creases. "Ooooh your make-up looks nice - can I take a picture of you using it for my insta? I'll keep your heart out of shot if you like." She stood me in front of Magda's geometric wallpaper and a golden Lama Figurine collection.

"What is it? Like a pouch?" asked Hayleigh.

I looked over Claire's shoulder as she uploaded my photo with her silk pouch, a flash of fashionable fabric. It actually made my outfit look edgier. I think I can pull this look off.

Check out my gorgeous friend Rebecca, rocking a #tribalprint #FHpouch … sewn by me! Ready to OWN work on Monday #FledglingHeart #WorkApparel #FHcommunity #FHfashion #BeTrueToYourHeart #homemade #LetsSew #FHsupport #FHmonday #HeartsAtWork Click on my Etsy link in bio!

"I've already sold 27!" Claire cooed, delighted with her new side hustle opportunities. "And people are sharing it! They're *soooo* easy to knock out too. I've made you a Ziggy Stardust lightning bolt one to wear on Monday… we can tag Bowie!"

After the pizzas were subjected to the customary uploading (Magda insisted on tagging Yasmin Khan, although from what I gather she has never been a pizza chef – "What will she do? De-tag a disability post? That would look terrible! I think we'll get away with it somehow, Becks."), we sat down to serious business.

Magda took her preordained post as chairperson. "Facebook and Twitter are already up in the Ks for comments and shares overnight. I bet it'll be viral by Monday. The bosses will know to expect you all in carrying your hearts. People all over are planning to do #FHmonday. Turns out so many were doing it secretly, and now they're feeling validated so they're sharing everything we're posting. Won't be long before we have Chrissy Teigan or someone Tweeting our corner."

"The back-in-my-day haters are getting shouted down in the threads," agreed Suneeta. "They just sound bitter that things weren't better for them before."

"They might even provide us with fridges to leave the hearts in?" interjected Hayleigh hopefully.

"Well, I'd like to keep my heart on me. I don't want it in a fridge where I can't tell if it's ok for myself. A fridge is great if you want one, but we shouldn't be forced to leave our hearts anywhere, even a fridge." I chose my words so carefully, but I could tell some of it still stung Hayleigh. She really wanted to believe in the cold, but there's no arguing with instinct.

"Others have been punished," warned Laura from HR. "There are protections in place, but they 'manage out' using Capability until people give up and leave. We've got to prove we can still work ok even with our hearts attached all day."

"They'll have to make some concessions, like cleaning up time. It's not fair to expect people to cope without their vital organs either. We only want a compromise." I reasoned.

"Loads of experts have already posted help on the threads for us," Magda said. "There's an Employment Lawyer who's obviously suffered herself with FH, and she's put tons of good stuff up as advice. The nice thing is, it is managing itself and we're not culpable for what she, or anyone else says. All we have to do is turn up and do a day's work."

"Here, here!" as the Bouvet clinked in Magda's flute glasses. I felt like Hamilton raising a glass to freedom and revolution. Monday is going to be intense.

The Fledgling Heart

Monday 26th November 2018

I'd been off long enough now, that I was looking forward to wearing my Hobbs dresses again to work. I knew I needed battle armour, and also the charm offensive, as Magda's camera phone was not going to let up all day.

Claire was the first to intercept me in the car park. "Oh, you wore it! You look *great!*" she babbled. "Let me get a shot in front of the glass doors… next to this palm tree... it looks like you could be somewhere glam if I crop out the pillars!" Snap. Snap. Snap. "…pre-sold 35 on Etsy! Everyone wants one! Might pack up this day job and live my dream gig, eh?"

The mortified looks from the receptionist was a jarring juxtaposition to Claire's enthusiasm. It was a long, arduous walk through New Business past the admin team at their desks. Feeling deeply awkward, I sidled into my swivel chair and logged onto my morning emails.

The first few hours went by quietly. My heart made a couple of audible complaints, which prompted some disdainful glances, but no one actually approached me. The rest of the time it leeched quietly and only spilled a few droplets of blood, thankfully hidden in the fabric of my Bowie pouch. *This going ok*, I told myself. As a collective, we only had one hiccup in the run-up to lunch time, with a screecher – loud and disturbing until our creative, Emma, got it reattached. Every so often, Magda or Claire would turn up, iPhones clicking, ironically drawing more attention to us than the hearts could ever hope to. Barbara the Borg avoided us entirely, which was just fine by me.

104

It was time to brave it and stretch my legs. I was dying for a pee and a coffee. Still trailing the remnants of my last conversation with a cheerful client, my mind was consumed in satisfaction, gratified to be lost in the solving of a problem again, and whirring deliciously. I wasn't paying attention to the figure appearing next to me at the percolator.

"Who do you people think you are, anyway?" Denise hissed venomously. Completely dumbfounded, I didn't reply, as I turned away from the coffee maker to face her.

"Don't stand there with your jaw open pretending, you selfish little upstart. How dare you expect us all to put up with *that*. It's *disgusting*." She spat acerbically.

"What do you suggest we do instead? Give up work? Or give up a pulse?" I regained from my initial surprise, but my temper was rising. I had to remember to check my composure, stay dignified, win her with logic...

"Where's your discipline? We never had such a sense of entitlement!" Her voice was curdled battery acid.

"You were entitled not to sacrifice your heart to a locker. That was your choice. If you felt your heart needed 'disciplining' that's your cross to bear, not mine. I'm not ditching my heart because you can't make peace with your regret."

"You self-righteous exhibitionist!"

"Well, I guess hostility is all we could hope to expect from someone with no heart." I was rather proud of this retort, until to my dismay, Barbara the Borg's voice appeared like a sudden puff of interrupting smoke.

"Rebecca, do you have a minute? I want a quick word." Her statement carried Barbara's signatory deadpan delivery. I shuffled along behind her on the long and very public journey to her office at the far side of the building. I detest her juvenile attempts at power play; imagine someone deliberately walking so fast that the person they've requested to join them has to run to keep up? She's so obvious it's loathsome. *I'm not performing your puppet routine by running around this office behind you, Barbara the Borg. I've done absolutely nothing wrong. In fact, I have had a GOOD DAY, all things considered.* I had to endure the wary stares of solidarity from Laura and Emma as we passed, and morbid curiosity from everyone else, reminiscent of the sorts of expressions drivers pull through their windows when they pass an accident on a motorway.

"Nice new throne, Barbara." I smiled breezily, maintaining the demeanour of the amicably oblivious while I nodded to the enormous black leather and chrome cathedra which had replaced her previous standard-issue, fabric-upholstered swivel chair, rationed out uniformly to the lowly plebs throughout the rest of the building. This peacock-like display of status was totally hilarious. And revealing.

"Keith Price from Reprographics gave it to me when they had a refurb," Barbara stated robotically. Keith is Denise's husband. Oh, that's just perfect. "How do think today has gone?" she moved on immediately to her chosen topic.

"Fine," I replied, only half truthfully but not missing a beat. "Apart from Denise giving me a load of grief, which you just saw. But that doesn't bother me. It's an issue for her. I'm sure I wouldn't be the first to mention her to you."

Barbara nodded. "Yes, I caught the end of that just now. Are you alright?"

What? What? The Borg is showing concern now? Was this some kind of new touchy-feely Well-Being initiative she's been forced to push? Maybe she'd been on a Bedside Manner training course.

This parade of inexplicable humanity threw me off and I lost my momentum. "Um, … yes, I'm fine. Is there a problem I don't know about?" Barbara is notorious for storing up the minor misdemeanours of her team like a poker player guarding a winning hand. Keeping her victim ignorant of her impending attack, until she is ready to strike.

"Not at all, I wanted to make sure you knew you had all our backing." She replied mechanically. "We want things to run smoothly, so let us know what we should do to make that happen. There are challenges we can't understand or fix unless people talk to me. I appreciate people might find it hard to talk to me. I know I'm not the most approachable personality. If it's easier for you, you can speak to Amanda." Amanda is Barbara's PA.

Barbara, for once, seemed entirely reasonable today. I don't know what's come over her. "I didn't realise staff welfare was in Amanda's remit."

"Well, it's not, officially. But she was happy to step up so that things run efficiently. Just like you have, actually. It's in all our interests. Recruiting is a gamble and it's expensive. I'd rather keep staff on than pay recruitment costs. It makes more sense to accommodate personal circumstances if we can."

After ten minutes, to my astonishment, I found myself questioning if the Borg had grown up into a decent manager after all, since the atrocious treatment of Magda during her cancer scare. It was a few years ago after all. Just because she's a robot it doesn't mean it's beyond her to want to do the right thing after a mistake, is it?

I'll give her one thing, she *is* effectual. It's a specialist aptitude of The Borg. My heart lead the concepts, and her Borg hive mind made them happen. We knocked out ideas for the rest of the afternoon, in an unlikely alliance of creative productivity. She's agreed to work unexpected cleaning times into the working day, if FH employees need to get changed or wipe up. She even suggested herself that one of the empty break out rooms could be made available to use when a heart starts squawking. Best of all, she will address the whole team on unacceptable conduct around their team mates, to pre-empt any Denises crawling out from under their holes again. I've underestimated Barbara. It was like watching Turin solve a Sudoku.

Unbelievably, I feel like Barbara and I worked together to pave the way for anyone who needs her to bend her machinelike ways in the future. We've done some good today, between us. I don't think we'll ever be mates, but I'll settle for a mutual admiration for our polar opposite strengths. My heart seemed to be in it too. Things are easier when you let yourself feel them properly.

By four in the afternoon, my head was nodding over my screen. Hayleigh was right, this was draining and exhausting, but I can't bear thinking about the alternative. This is infinitely preferable to turning my back on my precious heart, my treasure, who gives me focus, and purpose, and honesty to myself. Poor Denise. My day's work was done today, in more ways than one.

Paul's car was missing from our drive way as I pulled up to the house. This was odd, Paul normally finishes work before me and would've started prepping supper by now. Cooking after work is his decompression therapy. My stomach flipped and sank. *He's left. He couldn't take it.* I pushed the nonsensical intrusion away. *No, he hasn't. You're just tired. He's trying, like Barbara. Stop catastrophising, Becky.*

It was ghost-quiet as I turned my key in the door. I did not like it. My heart squirmed at my unease underneath its Bowie pouch. In the kitchen, there was no sign of Paul's typical evening sous chef preparations.

"Paul?" I called to the stairs. "Are you up there?"

Our room was in disarray. Disoriented, I strained to make sense of the scene. Planks of wood were sawn off at angles, to look like slats from under a bed. A wooden frame about the size of a small desk was pushed up against the side of our bed – my side. Paul's power tools were plugged in, ready for more use. He's not the DIY type. I stifled a giggle. *What's gotten into him?* His keys clunked in our front door as he arrived home.

"Are you upstairs, love? Have you seen my new build?" he sounded jubilant, and grinned when he found me laughing uncontrollably at the godawful chaos he had made of our room.

"What in the world is it?" I manage, between breaths. "What's made you get all crafty?"

109

"It's an IKEA upcycle thing I saw on Pinterest after I clicked on one of Magda's hashtags," he laughed. "You can't sleep downstairs forever, it's no good for you, for us… I miss you, Becks." He softened as he put down B&Q bags full of paints and foam tiles to wrap his arms around my waist. "It'll be a platform extension to our bed when it's done, so we can keep your heart happy in the night."

"Paul … I, I don't know what to say… I thought you had had enough, that you were too tired…" I should've known he had my back. He always has. "Thank you, Paul." I sighed, as I melted into his chest.

"I'm proud of you, love. I get it now, seeing you and Magda doing your thing. Come down and have a rest. I'll put the kettle on, and you can tell me how things went with Borg Bot today. I bet it was epic."

THE HARES OF
HORSENDEN
HILL

The Hares of Horsenden Hill

Horsa: Saxon chief and son of a King,

had but one daughter, Ealine Yilling.

Tales of her beauty far and wide

reached Bren of Brent, who made her bride.

She resisted the urge to scroll the history contained in her sleeping phone. Instead, Ealine tugged at the dwindling lock of hair from the base of her neck, where a patch of alopecia expanded. Flight-mode was switched on since the weekend, and she was even safer in this tunnel, where natural noise was bested by deafening subterranean smog, screeching at forced speed through the carriages. The air was compact and swaddling, carrying with it the cocooning relief that the notifications from the surface could not skewer her down here.

The tunnel also protected Kings Place and the rest of London's overground from the twisted knot forming in her stomach, which sooner or later, would require a notification of its own. Ealine did not know the man well, but she knew enough of him to judge she did not want his influence in her child's life. His notification would wait forever.

Of her mistreatment, Yilling sent.

Starling to Horsa, who, hell-bent

on avenging his only daughter,

challenged to duel Brent of Thames Water

Imperceptibly to the other St. Pancras commuters, a wash of secret shame shuddered through her. Behind Ealine's lids, she was back on his screen. A voice - only slightly distorted in that familiar timbre of connection buffering - from the dark of the room, sneers.

"So does this one have a voice? You don't usually let them talk mate."

Not a London accent, this must be one of his old Uni mates.

A round of fraternity sniggering.

"Are you *filming* me?"

This evening's load was heavy; she had more than usual to carry as the Tube pulled into Sudbury Town, but at least the hordes which typically pushed past were notably missing. And although Ealine enjoyed it once she got there, she was grateful that her Friday Boxercise class had been called off due to the pandemic. It was absurd, that the self-care cure for burn-out, should entail high-intensity calorie burning. Like a purge. Witches, punished, burnt at the stake.

In a chaotic frenzy, Ealine's editor at The Beholder had packed the writers off with extra devices, several phones, a work-only laptop for GDPR reasons, welfare questionnaires, hastily promising to see everyone on Monday's Zoom. Ealine was grateful she would earn her way through this. As the most senior writer on the Environment section of her paper, she knew she was one of the few who could work at full capacity without the standard dehumanising commute. She did not want a cigarette. She did not want a Friday drink. She was looking forward to the solitude.

To meet and cross at River Brent's ford.

There fought the two opposing Lords.

As if to dissuade her from her intentions for seclusion, Ealine's handbag vibrated an alert. Irritation turned to surprise, as she remembered she had switched her phone to flight-mode; receiving notifications was impossible. Perplexed, Ealine stopped walking, put her backpack down and fished around in her handbag to make sure she would not be disturbed again. Eerily, her device did indeed appear to be as she left it. Even odder still, was a rogue text message, which had managed to intrude in spite of her precautions. Without unlocking her phone to unleash the invasive text, Ealine could only see the first character of the message; a ghostly, stencilled silhouette of a rabbit or a hare.

Curiosity won, and Ealine followed the white rabbit down the hole: *[I know more about Hares than you can ever imagine. I can show how that feels. I can answer your questions and help with your labours. RSVP for details.]*

"Spam" Ealine immediately said out loud. But a deep movement within her had shifted subtly, and it cavilled at her silently, until Ealine had to read the proposal again. *Who is this? How do they know about my Environmental writing, or about my... labours?* Ealine switched the phone off.

Despite the backpack's weight, she decided not to head straight home. The evenings had recently turned brighter, and she never normally returned from work so early. Instead, Ealine walked away from the albatross of labels and debt in her rented apartment and headed along Whitton Avenue East,

114

turning left into Whittlers Woods to mull over the mystifying invitation.

Under those ancient oaks, the oppressive containment of the Tube wisped up into the rustling cool of afternoon leaves, following its own Will'o. Her backpack felt lighter. Her lungs filled with the ground's earthy musk, permeating up through the London clay and Dollis Hill gravel. Swishing canopies of fresh green brushed clear the air.

Bren was slain and Horsa wounded,

buried under the Hill now mounded.

Woodland soon smoothed into the grasslands of Horsenden East, where Ealine knew the cattle would not yet graze for another five months. Ahead, arose the broad, grassy summit of the Hill, an island protruding from an absent lake. A sudden queasiness floored her, either the beginnings of morning sickness or the prospect that the sprawling facade of Brent was awaiting, should she continue to mount it. She did not wish to see The Shard's phallic aspect any more than those unsolicited WhatsApp photos buried under recycle icons. Down here, she was shielded from that vista, and here encroached upon her an urge to press her stomach against the dry leaves and become flat. In a shallow dip of the long grass, she put her backpack of robotics down and sat, her back against it.

From the parapet in front of her, as if by way of example, she could see other beings burrowing too. The redwings sensed evening approaching and began to congregate to the safety of branches. A fresh molehill left a trace of another hunkering down. The kestrels had recently returned to form their territories disguised in the cavities of trees. To the birring, whirrup peeps of hidden parakeets, she lost an hour or two, until the sky changed hues.

Ealine noted that by now, whatever time it was, she would usually need an extra layer. But she felt no shiver under the lilac sky and the waning crescent moon's hanging smile. Dusk fell around her in a lavender haze, and an amaranthine vapour settled close to the ground, blanketing her further under her small valley.

T'was here the crone that mothered the maiden,

dug the green bolt-hole 'Ealing's Haven'.

A pair of long, black-tipped ears appeared, dancing just above the violet and mauve mists. They emerged from a shadowy existence in the last light fading from the day, and Ealine was surprised, but unmoved – responding to this March hare in the same way she noted the unseasonal temperature. It was curious, to say the least, that such a shy, hyper-vigilant creature would venture so close.

This was not the only trait to flag the specimen as a rarity. The hazelnut hare stood at least a metre tall. Her umber fur stood on end, enraged, and her eyes flashed in a crazed fury.

"Out, of my FORM." she hissed with bile-fuelled enunciation.

Again, Ealine, was not taken aback by this bizarity. "I'm sorry, your form?"

"My FORM," repeated the hare vehemently, twitching and ticking involuntarily. She clenched her paws up in front of her, low on her haunches in a boxer's stance. "My BED. Do you think I have spent my best March days, outrunning wolves, wild boar, and foxes, to have my form stolen from under my muzzle? Stand up and fight!"

"Leave her be," crackled an older voice. "Is your brain so waxing-mad that your eyes cannot see she is with leveret?" The voice came from another hare, crouched at the shoulders indicating her advanced age. Her ghost-fur was a luminous and immaculate winter snow.

"See, she has lined the form with her own plucked fur in preparation." The White Hare pulled Ealine up halfway out of the form and pushed her head aside to reveal a patch of slow-growing alopecia at the base of her neck, which subdued the March Hare, marginally. "We may have outrun those beasts, but Eostra hides from the Huntsmen and Hounds." The White Hare reprimanded, and at this, the March Hare shuddered.

"There's no fight in her anyway. I'd have boxed her ears before your waning whiskers interfered and no mistake," the March Hare muttered, casting a suspicious eye over the backpack abandoned in the form. Now she was distracted from fighting.

"Is *that* your basket of eggs?" The March Hare fell backwards into a guffaw, eyes streaming, unable to catch her breath.

117

The White Hare tolerated March's foible and turned to address Ealine for the first time. "Your defence is stillness and camouflage. Lie low in the form, with ears pressed flat to your back. Be still. Tuck your belly full of leveret to the ground." She croaked, "Better the Huntsman catches the fox, than either catch you."

Ealine shrank lower with the percipience. She knew at once, she had been granted a refuge denied to the other two hares, and this was the generosity of generations. She saw that the White Hare, beneath her milky-down, was scarred with attacks and narrow escapes.

"Eostre, you ken not of your own place, and have found yourself here without knowing how," began the White Hare crone. "If you outpace a slathering hound without your heart bursting forth from your ribs, your own kind will attempt to use your entrails for divination and have you skinned to line their collars. They will fudge your flesh into a Jugged Hare pie to feed their own. You may rest here but know that next comes the harvester to slice up your leveret. Then the men's mowers, turning your precious long grasses to silage, leaving you exposed and vulnerable. Hares are devoured in all ways, our modesty ravished, our leverets orphaned.

"Today, our Equinox, they stop. The men and machines are forced to allow you reprieve. So, what will you do Eostra? You hide here in the tussocks, that's what. And when you see the chance, leap. You have the strength of the maiden which came before you and the crone who comes after."

Unconsciously, Ealine's hand moved up to the base of her neck, searching out the small, familiar, expanding patch of alopecia. It was a nervous response she'd had since childhood, ripping out strands of hair to distract herself from anxiety. It had never grown back even in periods of peaceful living. The patch felt enormously bald, and Ealine realised it was proportionate to her rocketing distress over the past month.

But there was an itch beneath the bald skin, which seemed now to be scratching off in flakes under her nails. Underneath it, she detected with the pads of her fingertips, soft downy strands of fluff – could this be a recovery? It seemed to be sprouting at alarming speed though, as the rest of her hair fell out in clumps into her hands. The itch was spreading and irrepressible, a scorching burn forcing the entire covering of her body's skin to convulse with the sensation, like an overwhelming anaphylaxis.

Her jaw unhinged, dislocated, realigned, as her lens of vision was a concertina, an uncoiling spring uncurling around her head. The shells of her skull diverged and converged like tectonic plates, jutting her muzzle forward and her forehead back. Extending backwards, her ear buds were shooting into black-tipped stems. Sprouting hair intensified a fiery scald at Ealine's cheeks and above her mouth where weighted whiskers emerged to rebalance her disorientation. Ealine's previous anxiety processed itself into focus and purpose, as she became newly poised, acutely attuned to sights behind her and above her. The new awareness developed into an intuitive urge to lay flat against the ground.

A primordial, ancient restlessness stretched out her cracking limbs, and instinctively, without thinking, Ealine fell involuntarily into a downward-dog position. Mechanically, her spine snapped and elongated as if under the manipulation of an experienced chiropractor.

119

Inside, Ealine's entrails twisted into knots, addling the confusion and dread which ought to accompany this scene. Pain replaced terror. The agony distanced her from this spectacle in the same way mothers are removed from their indignities in labour. The pain is the threshold. Without trauma, the coming-of-age ceremony is incomplete. A memory flashed across her; a story about a butterfly retold in school assembly. An onlooker 'helped' the creature out of its cocoon. But because the butterfly had not squeezed itself through the tight tear, life-giving fluid was not wrought through its extremities, rendering it unable to unfold its wings to fly. Ealine was a spectator, watching herself being forced through a torturous portal, if she could endure it. She had no choice but to endure it, she was halfway down the birth canal.

Fresh blood gushed in to intoxicate new tissues with a soaring, heady agitation. Her marrow expanded and contracted; the sinews and muscles surrounding the lengthened bones, struggling to keep up with the pace, like unfurling petals striving to unfold to an unnaturally fast sunrise.

Gradually, Ealine recognised how rutted and crushed she had been in her preceding form, especially in her hind legs. With each stretch, Ealine noticed a conditioning, a straightening, a release. She was now lithe, supple, and loaded with a power ready to vault.

Her two new friends rushed to her side and helped Ealine up onto her hind legs. To take stock, the Three Hares embraced, and rather eccentrically for hares, nestled together in the same form, that they might fortify each other to daybreak.

Yilling's mother in the forest,

provided them with female fortress,

where her father had not done,

upon the Hill of Horsa Don.

Ealine woke stiff and midget-bitten to the first day of Spring and the first day of lockdown. She could not accept that her undertaking was a harmless dream conjured up by some meaningless junk mail. The encounter was raw enough that she was compelled to bear the veracity of her experience, and that the deliberate intention of its design was to prompt the offer's acceptance. She was no longer preoccupied with the genuineness of yesterday's cryptic summons. Instead, Ealine met an overpowering compulsion to seek out the sender. Newly determined, she carried her backpack home to her small, North London flat, ready to hunker down and lie low with her belly to the ground until it was her time to leap.

About the Author

Sarra Culleno is widely published, writing fiction and poetry for publication, performance, print, audiodramas, podcasts and radio. She was longlisted for the Cinnamon Press Pamphlet Prize, for Nightingale and Sparrow's Full Collections 2020, and nominated for Best of the Net 2020 by iambapoet.

Sarra is a frequent contributor to Fevers of the Mind, and to Alternative Stories and Fake Realities. She co-hosts Write Out Loud at Waterside Arts and performs as both guest and featured poet at numerous literary festivals.

You can follow Sarra's work on Social Media at:

YouTube – Youtube.com/user/sarra1978

Instagram – @sarracullenopoetry

Twitter – @sarra1978

Facebook – facebook.com/sarracullenopoetry

The Hares of Horsenden Hill first published by Mookychic Magazine and featured as part of the Hare Spell Trilogy audiodrama by Alternative Stories and Fake Realities

Oma's Song from The Legend of Baguley Brook was first published by Siren's Call Issue 50

Ab Zohr's Sonnet first appears as a reading on Alternative Stories and Fake Realities poetry podcast

Printed in Great Britain
by Amazon

72162361R00078